SUGAR-PUSS ON DORCHESTER STREET

OTHER RICOCHET TITLES

The Crime on Cote des Neiges by David Montrose
The Murder Over Dorval by David Montrose
The Body on Mount Royal by David Montrose
Waste No Tears by Hugh Garner

SUGAR PUSS

ON DORCHESTER STREET

Al Palmer

Véhicule Press

To Sean Edwin,
who didn't give a damn either!

Published with the assistance of the Canada Council for the Arts,
the Canada Book Fund of the Department of Canadian Heritage,
and the Société de développement des entreprises culturelles du
Québec (SODEC).

Series editor: Brian Busby
Special assistance: Asa Boxer
Adaptation of original cover: J.W. Stewart
Typeset in Minion by Simon Garamond
Printed by Marquis Printing Inc.

LIBRARY AND ARCHIVES CANADA CATALOGUING
IN PUBLICATION

Palmer, Al, 1913-1971
Sugar-puss on Dorchester Street / Al Palmer ; Will Straw
(introduction).

(Ricochet)
ISBN: 978-1-55065-349-6

I. Title. II. Series: Ricochet books

PS8531.A424S84 2013   C813'.54   C2013-902062-4

Published by Véhicule Press, Montréal, Québec, Canada
www.vehiculepress.com

Distribution in Canada by LitDistCo
www.litdistco.ca

Distributed in the U.S. by Independent Publishers Group
www.ipgbook.com

Printed in Canada on FSC certified paper

INTRODUCTION

Will Straw

I bought my first copy of Al Palmer's 1949 novel *Sugar-Puss on Dorchester Street* sometime in the mid-1980s, at the Salvation Army Thrift Store on rue Notre-Dame in Montreal. Even in those days, copies of post-war Montreal pulp novels were becoming scarce, but it was not impossible to stumble across them in second-hand shops or church basement rummage sales. *Sugar-Puss* sat on the Sally Ann's shelves alongside a copy of Palmer's only other book, the 1950 part-guide, part-exposé *Montreal Confidential*. I snapped up them both for less than the cost of a greasy spoon coffee.

Sugar-Puss was published in two editions, with different covers, and for a long time I had only the second, intended for the U.S. market, with its slightly more sleazy illustration. The title character stands in profile on a neon-lit street – Dorchester Street, a sign tells us – leaning against a building and smoking a cigarette. The art recalls the style of Will Eisner, who drew the influential 1940s comic book *The Spirit*, but it also exaggerates the female character's anatomy in a manner typical of low-end pulp magazines. The female on the cover might well have been a woman of the night, and the well-dressed man looking at her seems to be working up to a lewd proposition. No comparable scene appears in the novel and the book is clearly straining to appear more naughty than it is. The tagline, above the book's title, reads "Racy, Risqué – But Warmly Human. An Unforgettable Story".

Though it had yet to sell a copy, the first edition of *Sugar-Puss on Dorchester Street* carried the cover blurb "The Best Selling Novel About Montreal". The cover image for this Canada-only edition was slightly cleaner than that which followed it, though only slightly. We see the book's heroine, Gisele Lepine (the novel doesn't bother with French accents) in a crimson dress, carrying her suitcase along Montreal's downtown nightclub strip. Has she just arrived in Montreal – from what the back cover calls "the cool clean air of her Laurentian village"? Or is she fleeing the city to go home, as she threatens to do at least once in the novel when life gets too intense?

In a grand tradition that reaches back at least a couple of centuries and runs through literature high and low, *Sugar-Puss on Dorchester Street* tells a story of innocence challenged and corrupted by the big city. Facing a monotonous life in the rural Quebec town of St. Christophe, Gisele has clung to memories of a childhood family visit to Montreal and secretly set aside money with which to fund her flight to the city. Conveniently, she has spent her teenage summers serving tourists at a local resort, where she learned to speak flawless English (and to handle the unwanted advances of rich men.) On her arrival in Montreal, she is plunged into a world of English-speaking journalists and chorus girls transplanted from New York. As in so many of the post-war Montreal pulp novels written in English, the only Francophone characters in *Sugar-Puss on Dorchester Street* are police officers and the occasional gangster.

Gisele's love interest is Jimmy Holden, the impeccably tailored night-life-and-crime reporter for the *Chronicle* newspaper. It's not hard to see Holden as effortlessly standing in for Al Palmer himself. Like Holden, Palmer was by all accounts a well-liked, talented big-city columnist who moved between the night-club and police beats and occasionally combined these. When the novel puts him in jeopardy, Holden considers an offer to work for a newspaper in Florida. We know that Palmer himself had gone to Florida in 1949 to work for *the Key West Citizen*, writing both *Sugar-Puss on Dorchester Street* and *Montreal Confidential* there. He returned to Montreal shortly thereafter.

Al Palmer covered Montreal's lively night-time culture for almost three decades. Like New York City columnists before him – Walter Winchell or Ed Sullivan, for example – Palmer was as much one of the emblematic characters of the Montreal night as he was its chronicler. Born in 1913, Palmer spent his early professional life writing for suburban Montreal newspapers and covering sports for a variety of outlets. For most of his career he worked for two of Montreal's English-language dailies. At the *Montreal Herald,* he wrote the column "Cabaret Circuit", then moved to the *Gazette* in 1957, writing a similar column, "Our Town", until illness slowed him down in the late 1960s. He died in 1971, just as Montreal's post-Expo slump and the rise of disco music had eradicated much of the night-time culture in which Palmer lived and flourished. Once the centre of Montreal's nightlife, Dorchester Street, as Montrealers of a certain vintage know, became a boulevard in 1955, and twenty-two years later was renamed Boulevard René-Lévesque.

Alongside his work as mainstream reporter/columnist, Palmer turned up in publications of lesser stature. In 1939, Palmer contributed the column "Montreal Backstage" to the short-lived and crudely-produced Toronto-based tabloid *The National Tattler.* He ceded that position in 1940 to the mysterious "S. R. Martin", who also wrote about Montreal night-life for several years in the slightly more respectable Toronto gossip sheet *Hush*. In 1952, Palmer contributed a regular feature, "Hello Montreal", to the pocket-sized weekly Montreal magazine *Encore*, about which little is known. (Copies of *Encore* are preserved in the papers of the "Comité de moralité publique", the municipal reform organization in which future Montreal mayor Jean Drapeau made his name.) Al Palmer's personal papers and a rich inventory of photographs from his collection are available for consultation in the Al Palmer fonds at the Concordia University Archives in Montreal.

The night-life which Palmer chronicled in his books and columns is remembered more fondly today by Anglophone Montrealers than by their Francophone counterparts. Anglophones, in so much of the English-language writing covering this time, float through a world of nightclubs and cabarets disconnected from the political repression and degraded public life which reform-minded Francophones were struggling to overthrow. In 1950, the year after *Sugar-Puss* was first published, the Caron Inquiry into corruption and commercialized vice in Montreal was launched, following pressures from the newspaper *Le Devoir* and municipal reformers like Pax Plante and Jean Drapeau. In that year, as well, Quebec Premier Duplessis carried on a campaign against obscenity, while Montreal's city council passed by-laws prohibiting women from wearing "indecent clothing" in public spaces. Of course, none of this appears in Palmer's book. The Runyonsesque, downtown Montreal of *Sugar-Puss on Dorchester Street* has more than its share of danger and exploitation, but we read the book tantalized by a world of late-night frolics and mid-day liquid breakfasts.

When I moved first to Montreal in 1978 night-life chroniclers in Al Palmer's mould were still flourishing in the city's media. Figures like Thomas Schnurmacher, Michel Girouard and Douglas "Coco" Leopold turned up at discos, mingled with their era's version of café society and spilled it all the next morning, in print or over the airwaves. In Montreal, as in most cities, this sort of night-life columnist has disappeared, and entertainment gossip survives mostly in features on global celebrities pieced together by editors from wire services and websites. Gone are the nightclubs in which a city's elite sat alongside criminal low-lifes, aspiring scene-makers and journalists, like Al Palmer, who made this world their professional domain.

PREFACE

Dorchester Street spews out almost within shadow of the Harbour Bridge in Montreal's slummy, crummy East End. Her spawning ground is wedged solidly between vermin-ridden tenements where French and English meet – but do not blend – and the greasy waters of the St. Lawrence River.

From this point, as if seeking escape from the dreary frustration of her birthplace, she threads her way on a littered ribbon of asphalt. Heading westward she bisects the one-time world-famed Red Light district which pollutes the air just east of St. Lawrence Main; hurriedly skirts the Jewish ghetto at Clarke Street and pauses only after passing the sordid commercialism of Bleury.

Here her pace slackens and, seemingly on tiptoes, she passes between the quiet dignity of St. Patrick's Church and the ramshackle walls of the Jesuit College.

She continues at a leisurely pace to the summit of Beaver Hall Hill. Here she squirms past the office building on her left and draws a deep breath of fresh air as she finds herself in the centre of the Place. Pausing only to note that the air of aristocracy has departed from the moss-covered buildings, she hurries past the iron chains that bind the grassy plot in the island.

Further west, at University, she passes between a modern aviation building and a club for venerable old gentlemen. The club, she muses, seems to be standing rigidly at attention as if on guard against further invasions of its serenity.

Later she wends her way over the bridge to Metcalfe Street where statues of saints atop St. James Basilica look reproachfully down. The shadow cast by the largest office building in the Empire shrouds her in shade, giving the area a cloistered look.

Further, at Dominion Square, she lingers to look at the idlers on the grassy plots. The plots, she recalls with a tinge of nostalgia, once laid a green mantle over the city's graveyard.

Westwards she skirts between one of the oldest and newest hotels and finds herself amid her favourite surroundings. Here, just west of Peel Street, the best families built their elaborate homes in the not-too-distant past. Not too distant? The impressive fronts remain but the vulgar signs that scream of tourist accommodations out-shout the ornate workings of the fronts and serve only as a contrast to what was a once prosperous era.

Today the families have gone. Commercialism has replaced the art of gentle living. Dollar-hungry landlords elbow out those who would preserve the dignity of a once-exclusive section.

Leaving her bitter-sweet memories she travels west, past Guy Street and slowly wends her way past Victorian mansions now reeking of shabby gentility until she reaches Atwater. Once west of the city limits she loses herself in middle-class squalor. This is Dorchester Street. For this Gisele Lepine traded the cool cleanliness of a Laurentian village.

THE CHARACTERS

Gisele Lepine, a farmerette with a personal five-year plan: "I wonder what he will do. And I wonder what I will do – if he will do what I am wondering he will do."

Jimmy Holden, a reporter who would much rather buy clothes than eat – and frequently did. "When you leave Montreal, Sugar Puss, you aren't going anywhere."

Gaston Courtney, a nightclub operator with other interests – including Gisele. "Too many persons get married for better or for worse– but not enough for good."

Jim Schultz, a bistro bossman who mangled expensive cigars – and the King's English. "You're just as safe as if you were in yah mudda's arms. Safer – unless yah mudda's got cauliflower ears."

Sammy Hoffman, a newspaperman whose sole reasons for living were wine and women. The song he left strictly to the birds. "Writers' cramp is what you get trying to eat on a reporter's salary."

Trixie, a hoofer who had what it took to take what they had. "Pa said he named me after a pet mongrel who died. Ma said it was after a burlesque broad."

Diane, a chorus girl whose platinum hair felt better on Sammy's shoulder. "He's got something. Can't be money. He borrowed cab fare to bring me home this morning."

Mike, a cab driver who knew all the answers – he had heard all the questions.

Kuo, a Chinese chauffeur who spoke a half-dozen languages but couldn't find the answer in any one of them.

CHAPTER ONE

Tired bed springs creaked their protest as Gisele raised herself to one elbow in order to get a broader view of the attic which had been her bedroom for almost as long as she could remember.

Her gaze slowly wandered about the room to finally fall upon the gaudy patch work quilt draped over the chipped enamel bed. The quilt served as a constant reminder of *Grand'mere* Arsenault's long and active life. Gisele recalled that it was only two days after her beloved grandmother had sewn the final stitch that the *Bon Dieu* had called and, as if it was the most natural thing in the world to do . . . she died.

Grand'mere had patiently worked the bed spread with aged but nimble fingers as a wedding gift for Gisele and Pierre. "Come '*Ti-Chou*," she would cackle. "You need a man. Winters are long and cold in Quebec and one needs warmth. One also needs many children to help work many acres. Soon the farm will be Pierre's. We must hurry."

Many times, Gisele had prayed that the old lady would cease urging her to marry Pierre. She realized, not without misgivings, that his position would soon be difficult. The village would be curious.

"*Pauvre Pierre*," she thought. "When I tell him he will be most upset. But then . . . why tell him?"

She had long since been aware that the entire village was anxiously awaiting the day when she and Pierre would stand side by side before beloved Pere Racine – thereby uniting two of the oldest families in the region.

Centuries ago the Lepines and the Cotes, along with many others, had set forth from their native Normandie to seek a new life in a New France. The hardships, the privations and the dangers they withstood is written in blood on the pages of Canadian history.

The group headed by the Lepines and Cotes chose as their home a densely wooded wilderness infested by savage wild life and equally savage Iroquois. They survived both and, with typical Gallic devoutness, credited their survival to the intervention of St. Christopher, patron saint of the traveler, and later named the settlement in his honor.

Although realizing the significance of the marriage, Gisele knew she could not go through with it. She fervently wished she could love Pierre – but knew that was not possible. If she could do so it would all be so simple.

But then, slow-thinking Pierre did not measure up to her expectations of a lover. He smelled cow. His dirty fingernails sickened her. His table manner revolted her. Ruefully, she thought, he reminded her too much of her father.

She recalled the height of Pierre's love-making with amusement. It had taken place deep within the nearby woods during one of their regular Sunday afternoon strolls.

Pierre had suddenly pleaded for proof of her love. Breathing heavily he implored her to allow him to examine her.

She regarded him coolly at first but finally consented. With awkward gropings his calloused hands fumbled with her clothing until in a fit of desperation, he had torn them from her body.

His clumsiness kindled her temper to a white hot pitch. She set upon him belaboring his head and chest with her fists. She screamed, "*Cochon! Cochon!*" after his retreating figure then threw back her head and laughed hysterically at her nakedness in the forest.

Fully a week had passed before Pierre summoned sufficient courage to call at the Lepine home. When he did so Gisele accepted his apology and neither mentioned the incident again. Nor did Pierre attempt any further love making.

Neither, she realized rather bitterly, did any of the other youths of the village. She was Pierre's by common assent . . . that was Quebec.

The importance of the day at hand excited her. She sank back on the pillow and let her mind wander over the events of the past five years. There was Jackie of course. He was a co-median at the lodge where she was employed as a waitress.

After several futile attempts to lure her into his room Jackie had decided that she was, as he put it, "a sweet kid." His discovery led him to appoint himself as guardian of her morals and chief adviser of her behaviour. "Kid," he once said, "if you don't sell it – sit right on it. Don't go givin' nothin' away."

Gisele did neither.

Breakfast noises drifting up from the kitchen made further reminiscence impossible. Leaping agilely from the bed she walked cat-like to the cracked wash basin which stood on the hand-hewn dresser. She pulled the flannel night gown over her head and flexed her muscles languidly.

She was eighteen and looked two years older. Her hair was blue-black and pointed to a widow's peak on a smooth forehead. Her eyes were large and softly brown as was her skin thereby hinting of a strain of Basque blood. Her breasts were large and firm; a legacy of her Norman ancestry. Long legs tapered off from well-rounded thighs to shapely ankles. Her feet were small and beautifully formed as are those of most French Canadian women.

She looked at the date on the food store calendar. June 24. The Feast of St. Jean Baptiste, patron saint of French Canada. The date was heavily circled in black. To Gisele the dare symbolised her personal Day of Liberation. This day marked the completion of her personal five-year plan. This day she would bid a not too sorrowful adieu to St. Christophe-sur-le-Lac and the limited life it offered.

Her mind raced back through the half-decade when the Lepines brought the thirteen-year-old Gisele for her first and last visit to Montreal. Excitedly they told her that to see a St. Jean Baptiste parade was an experience she would not forget for many years.

They had gesticulated with *habitant* enthusiasm as float followed float in rapid succession each portraying a significant event in the history of French Canada. The gaiety of the crowd and the breath-taking spectacle of the parade inevitably provided them with enough material about which to talk throughout the long winter on their tiny farm.

But neither the colorful floats nor the enthusiasm of her parents impressed Gisele. Instead she gazed with envy at the smartly clad women and neatly tailored men who lined Sherbrooke Street.

She gazed in rapture at the tall apartment buildings standing majestically on each side of the street, and stared in awe at occupants of the sleek cars parked on the side streets waiting for the parade to pass.

It was then that Gisele's young-old mind made itself up. Immediately the neat and pleasant farm was mentally transformed into one of bleak desolation. This was where she belonged, she decided. How long would take? Five years, at least. This was no idle day dream of an adolescent, but a decision to which she clung with feverish tenacity.

Almost desperately she promised herself that she would return to take her place among these people. She, too, would ride in one of those sleek automobiles and perhaps even live in a towered apartment block on Sherbrooke Street.

In five years she would be eighteen. French Canadian girls matured fast and she realized that if she were not married by that her family would never cease reminding her if the fact. No. That was not for her. She would come to Montreal and leave Pierre among his stupid cattle.

There was so much to do she wondered if five years was a sufficient length of time. First she must learn to speak English; that was all-important. She must also earn some money. This, too, would be difficult in a village where a thirteen-year-old girl was expected to help her mother in the kitchen and her father with the chores until she married.

Perhaps her parents could be talked into sending her to school in the city. The futility of this struck her almost as she thought of the possibility. They would never allow her to leave the farm. Of course, she could enlist the aid of kindly Father Racine who would no doubt influence them if he saw the possibility of Gisele entering a convent to finally emerge prepared to take the vows of a nun.

But even if this plan were to succeed, she thought dismally, her life in a Montreal convent would be even more firmly cloistered than her life on the farm.

Her thoughts were interrupted by Papa Lepine as he clutched her arm and started down Guy Street in the midst of the hurrying crowd.

A fine rain was falling as they reached the corner of St. Catherine. The moisture crowned each of the thousand lights with a rainbow-tinted halo. Gisele was speechless with wonder as she gazed enchanted at the shining pavement and the reflections made by the neon signs as they switched from red to green in multi-colored splashes of light.

CHAPTER TWO

They turned east from Guy Street and started toward the brilliant glow that was Peel and St. Catherine.

"Gisele, my little cabbage, can it be that you are frightened by the city?"

Her father's voice came to her as if through a haze. She jerked her head upwards to face him. "No, no, Papa. It is just that it is all so big and . . . so strange and noisy."

Mama Lepine looked fondly at her daughter. "*Eh, bien*, Gisele. Papa will take us to a restaurant and for the first time in many days, we will not be required to wash the dishes."

Smiling at her little joke she held her daughter's hand more firmly and walked as if heading for high adventure.

Although by no means familiar, Montreal was not entirely a strange city to the elder Lepines. It was here that they spent their honeymoon and, they recalled, had been happy to leave at the end of a single week.

Not that their honeymoon had been anything but happy. It served, however, to prove to them that they necessarily were country people.

Their country-bred ears had rebelled against the never-ending noise. The lofty buildings and the streams of traffic had both confused and frightened them. A half hour's walk along crowded pavements inevitably filled them with a longing for the tranquillity of the farm.

Then again, the cheap room at a Dorchester Street tourist home left much to be desired. The place was a far cry from the bridal suite for which they hoped when leaving for the city. The house was frequently filled with tourists all of whom it appeared were constantly in the middle of an alcoholic celebration.

Then, too, there were many over-painted young girls who rented rooms by the hour and entertained steady parades of young men. None, they noticed, had luggage. Even to the unsophisticated minds of Paul and Marie Lepine the purpose of these visits was obvious.

One day Lepine encountered a permanent guest at the house returning from the tobacco shop on Peel Street. He was halfway up the stairs when he first saw her. She wore heavy make-up and sported a satin dress which left no doubt whatsoever of her sex.

"*Pardonnez-moi*," Lepine said as he moved aside.

"Okay, Hayseed," she answered with a smile.

Upstairs in the room he discussed the incident with Marie. Neither could interpret the word "hayseed" and Marie held firmly to the belief that Paul had not heard correctly. Both agreed, however, that the woman held her virtue lightly.

Marie was first to voice what both were thinking. "Can it be Paul, that we are staying at a place where there is also living persons whose morals are loose?" Her eyes widened in fright as she realized the full meaning of her statement.

"It is quite possible, *Bebe*." Paul replied with a forced air of nonchalance.

"Then, Paul, it is most necessary the we pack our things and move as quickly as it is possible. *Non!* But immediately."

She moved about the room with fluttering motions as if on the verge of panic. Paul reached out and grabbed her by the wrist pulling her to him. She fell into his arms kissing him fiercely.

He rubbed his chin on her forehead and softly whispered, "Let's go home, *Bebe*."

She looked beseechingly into his eyes. "Please, Paul. The city is not for us."

The prospect of returning home raised their spirits and they laughed at the seriousness of the situation just a moment previous.

Paul freed one hand and snapped off the light leaving the room in darkness except for the blue-ish tinge which crept in on either side of the shaded window.

Later they packed and discussed their stay in the city. Each felt ever so slightly wicked at having spent a week in what they were now convinced was the largest brothel in the entire city.

"Perhaps it would be wise not to mention this escapade to *Monsieur le Cure*," Paul said with laughter. "I am sure *le bon pere* would not approve of our choice of lodgings."

The incident became one of the many sweet secrets they shared and now, as they walked down St. Catherine Street with their first-born between them, Paul smiled at his wife.

"Perhaps we should have christened this little one 'Dorchester'."

"Paul!" Mama said sharply as a deep blush bloomed unseen beneath her heavy tan.

The trend of her parents' conversation escaped Gisele. She was walking as if through a fairyland and was busily planning places to visit when she returned. She looked with open admiration at passers-by for some time before noticing that many smiled strangely at the Lepines.

Confused for a moment she smiled in return. Then she realized the smiles were directed at their appearance. There was little doubt that their clothes were out of place. With sinking heart she knew they were farmers and, worse still, looked the part.

Papa's clothes even gave off a strong smell of the barn, she noted.

At first a wave of panic engulfed her as she sought frantically to escape the ridiculing stares. Her father's boots . . . not one man had she noticed wearing boots. All wore shoes . . . highly polished shoes. Her father's ill-fitting blue serge suit and stripped shirt stood out in the crowd as conspicuously as any of the electric signs under which they passed.

Her mother's home made cotton dress and her own cheap outfit, set off by a pair of black lisle stockings, filled her with humiliation. She bit her lower lip to keep back the flood of tears welling inside. She fought back the urge to run and hide her face in shame.

Shame? She realized she was ashamed of her parents and of herself. Frantically she vowed to ask the Blessed Virgin's forgiveness a hundred times.

But if the Lepines were aware of the curious stares directed at them they showed no signs. Happily – almost jubilantly – Papa steered his brood into a modern restaurant near the corner of Peel Street.

The place was a garish nightmare set in red leather and chrome. It boasted of a soda fountain running the full length of the room and a bevy of well-trained waitresses resplendent in starched white uniforms.

Gisele noticed that the restaurant was crowded almost to capacity and that every head seemed to turn and that everyone seemed to stare in their direction. They followed a trim efficient hostess to a booth.

As the three of them were handed a menu with a professional air, Gisele saw a young man nudge his companion and nod in their direction. Her cheeks burned as they faced each other again with knowing smiles.

What Papa had planned as a pleasant diversion for his daughter turned out to be the most miserable experience in her short memory.

She squirmed with embarrassment when her father ordered in halting broken English – only to discover the waitress spoke French fluently.

His every action added to her discomfort. His loud voice attracted even more attention. For a moment she considered seeking refuge in the ladies' room but hadn't the courage to run the gauntlet of many staring eyes.

Instead she lowered her eyes and concentrated on finishing her ice cream as rapidly as possible. Meanwhile, the Lepines chatted gaily . . . oblivious of everyone except themselves.

Gisele almost cried with relief when at last they reached the street. She stood for a moment fascinated by the signs and sounds of the city and solemnly swore to herself that she would return.

All through the long bus ride home she feigned sleep to avoid the multitude of questions her parents would ask her. And, once inside the farm house, she bid them a dutiful 'good night' and ran upstairs to her room. Then, for the first time, she cried herself to sleep.

From then on she tactfully refused all invitations to accompany her parents to Montreal. She insisted that it was only fair the younger children be given the opportunity of witnessing a St. Jean Baptiste parade.

CHAPTER THREE

This time it will be different Gisele told herself in the mirror. "Five years is a long time to wait but I know it will be worth it."

Proudly she reviewed her accomplishments since that disastrous St. Jean Baptiste Day five years ago.

Almost from that day when she returned home to cry herself to sleep she had studied English. Soon after she found a job as a dish washer at Auberge d'Eau Claire, a rambling all-year-round tourist resort on the outskirts of the village.

There she practiced English until she spoke it with only the slightest trace of an accent. She soon graduated from the kitchen to the dining room where she became the favorite waitress of the wealthy guests.

She studied their mannerisms and copied their clothes. Most of them were Americans who tipped lavishly and, by dint of careful saving, Gisele soon accumulated sufficient money to put her plan into action.

An uncanny ability to ward off advances from the male guests without injuring their pride earned her their respect. She handled the most irritable women guests with ease, and soon collected a wardrobe of clothes "which I just can't cram into my luggage, Gisele," from many of them.

She was none too happy about the prospect of leaving the lodge. It had been an escape from the dreary routine of the farm.

As she finished her packing she looked proudly at the handsome luggage which held her clothes. It was a farewell gift from Jackie the comic who presented it to her after an impressive ceremony.

She had kissed him lightly on the forehead in thanks

whereupon he immediately fell flat on his back. The staff laughed heartily as he did so – but then they laughed at almost everything he said or did.

She picked up her flannel night gown from the floor and hung it in the closet. None of her home made dresses was included in her luggage. She was indeed thankful to the lodge.

When she had first broken the news to her parents about accepting a job at the rambling resort there had been a scene. Papa pointed out the dangers of working in a place where so many men gathered without their wives.

He cautioned that it was common gossip in the village that some of the drunken parties held there were little less than orgies. The lodge had a bad name and did not Pere Racine warn the villagers about the place from his pulpit only last Sunday?

Gisele compromised by promising to return home after work each evening. She had kept the promise faithfully. The fact, and the generous amount of her earnings she contributed to the household, lessened – but did not eliminate – their opposition to her working.

That was the first crisis the Lepines had had with their first born. Gisele drew a deep breath. "Here, now, will be the second."

Descending to the kitchen she immediately began helping her mother with the breakfast table. The rest of the children would be down shortly and she had decided not to make her departure known until they had finished eating and had disappeared from the house.

First to arrive was 16-year-old Jacques. He fastened a heavy belt around his faded blue denims and, teeth gleaming, shouted greeting to his mother and sister.

Jacques' arrival at meal times never failed to break the monotony. His unfailing good humor and high spirits were a source of amazement to both his family and the neighbors.

Unlike the average farmer's son Jacques was never given to moody spells. He seemed to move about in a world all his own. He would perform the most disagreeable chores without complaint but nevertheless was still a source of worry to his sister.

"Too handsome," she thought. "He will break many hearts in this village. Perhaps, too, his own heart will be broken. He is the type who will fall heavily in love."

Papa Lepine soon entered from the barn and took his place at the head of the table. He glanced around his ever-growing family and said grace with a blessing for each of his progeny: Gisele, Jacques, Andre, Annette, Gaston, Pierre, Juliette and "*Bebe*" Jean who at four years was the pride and joy of the household.

Gisele waited impatiently until the last of the younger children had finished breakfast and, with joyful whoops, scattered out into the sunshine.

She coughed nervously. "Papa."

"*Oui* Gisele," he answered without looking up.

"I am going to Montreal."

The silence which followed was finally broken by Mama. "*Mais certain,* Gisele. You are going to see the St. Jean Baptiste parade. *N'est ce pas?*"

Conscious of her parents' eyes upon her she replied, perhaps a bit too casually. "No. I plan to live there."

Her mother's face blanched. Papa stared in silence for a moment then carefully placed his knife and fork on his plate.

"Gisele, *bébé*," his voice was low. "Can it be that you are in trouble? Is it that you wish to tell your parents of some condition which you find yourself in and wish to escape . . ."

Gisele's face softened and she fondly took her father's gnarled fingers in her own. "No Papa, that is not the case." She smiled at the expression of relief as it spread across his weather-beaten face.

Mama Lepine looked steadily at her daughter. "Is it that you are not happy here?" Her voice was flat and toneless and Gisele thought she detected a thread of frustration gathering her words into the halting sentence.

Conscious of the despair in her mother's eyes Gisele tried a fresh approach. Lightly and with exaggerated gaiety she said, "I am going to the city for one reason. I believe I will prefer life there to what it is here at the farm. It is very simple. I want to live like city people. I . . . belong there."

Lepine shrugged his shoulders in a helpless gesture. It is inevitable, he thought. Always one of the younger people of the village grew up hating the farm. It was a pity that they were always the more intelligent ones.

He recalled that during the war years familiar faces would disappear almost daily. The young men had left to join the services and the girls had followed to work in war plants. "And why not," he asked himself. "What has the land to offer these young hopefuls. Little more than years of backbreaking labor as one struggles with the soil and, in the end, a house filled with hungry children and a meagre income on which to feed them.

When he was a boy it was the accepted thing for the young men to marry and to clear a few acres for their bride. He could not remember one of his friends who could speak a word of English. Yet here he sat with his two oldest children both of whom spoke the language fluently and with but little accent.

He doubted if Jacques would take over the farm. He, too, resembled Gisele. Both were intelligent youngsters and, he realized sadly, neither had the personality to be content with the dreary offerings of the farm life.

Suddenly he found himself envying Gisele. Perhaps if he were her age and possessed her talents he, too, would have left the farm. He would have thrown over the land and the heritage of countless Lepines and made his way to the city.

"Silly fool," he thought. At her age he was well on his way to what he is today; a worn out, youngish-old-man who had given his years and his youth in cultivating the minute part of Quebec Province which his fore-fathers had wrested from the wilderness and had claimed as their own.

Gisele sat in silence her hands folded in her lap, looking tenderly at her parents. Mama, it seemed, had been continually pregnant ever since she could remember.

Mirrored in her mother's face she saw a picture of herself as she might become. A farm wife: first a slave to a husband then to an ever-growing family. Wrinkles and lines came early to the faces of farm wives.

A constant round of labor pains and back-breaking toil in the fields gradually took its toll until the body shuddered its protest and all that remained was a wicker rocking chair and a patchwork quilt to fashion for an ungrateful grandchild.

Such had been Grand'mère Arsenault's life. Such was the present pattern of her mother's. But that will not be mine. She almost screamed the thought aloud.

Jacques startled the silent group by shouting, "Bus leaves in twenty minutes – bus leaves in twenty minutes." He droned the words in a fain imitation of a train announcer's voice.

Gisele thanked him with her eyes. There was too little time for lengthy farewells and she was impatient to get away. Each minute the ancient house became increasingly unbearable.

CHAPTER FOUR

As the huge bus nosed its way into the Dorchester Street Terminal Gisele thought she would burst with elation. She looked excitedly out of the window at the crowded streets. She saw one couple dressed as she and her parents must have dressed five years ago.

Their appearance, she thought, must create something of a sensation. We, too, looked just as strange as that. It was almost unbelievable. The memory of that day gave her an uncomfortable feeling so she picked up her grips and hastily walked from the depot, her head held high with determination.

Turning west from the terminal she stared fascinated at the row of tourist room signs stacked one against the other as far as the eye could see on Dorchester Street.

Choosing one she believed to be both clean and cheap she walked boldly in and headed for the janitor's apartment which, she saw by the sign, was on the second floor.

Halfway up the dimly-lit stairway, she almost collided with a coarse, full-blown blonde whose clinging dress accentuated, rather than revealed, her ample curves.

"*Pardonnez-moi*," Gisele said politely.

"Okay, Hayseed," the blonde answered.

Later in her room Gisele pored over every Montreal newspaper she could buy at the terminal news stand. Those offering waitress jobs were circled and set aside. This done, she sat on the window seat and looked down three storeys on to the crowds strolling below.

The excitement of the day added to her fatigue and she finally stretched full length upon the bed and fell into a deep dreamless sleep despite the noise of traffic welling up from the busy street.

She awoke with a start, bewildered by her strange surroundings, and for a brief moment sat on the bedside pondering her wisdom in coming to the city. To return was out of the question even though a sense of loneliness beat down upon her and for once, she longed for the familiarity of home.

Finding employment proved no problem whatsoever. The first place she applied, a cheap restaurant on St. Catherine east of Bleury, hired her on the spot.

The proprietor ran his eyes over her obvious charms and hired her then and there. He was a huge man. His stomach bulged over his belt. His face was fat and florid and a greasy texture stood out from his skin.

Stubby fingers topped with blackened finger nails ran through his oily hair. "Not bad. Not bad." He told himself.

Gisele set about waiting on tables after changing into a crisp white uniform. The uniform was the only thing crisp . . . or white for that matter . . . in the place.

The customers, she decided, were not quite so select a group as were those she served at the mountain lodge.

She noticed that her employer's eyes seldom left her as she hurried back and forth between the tables and the kitchen.

The owner drummed his fingers on the top of the cash register. "She's a proud one," he told himself, "this will take a bit of time."

The "bit of time" he figured on lasted three days. On the morning of the fourth day he cornered her in the tiny kitchen. "Come to Poppa," he grunted, his eyes wide with excitement.

Gisele was carrying a deep bowl of special salad in her right hand. She was wondering how anyone could stomach the mushy collection of kitchen scrap when she heard him. In her left hand she held a bowl of *soupe au pois Canadien Francais* – a heavy pea soup so thick it was close to being a solid.

Her employer's hands reached her waist – his fingers dug deeply into her ribs. "Hey, kid," his voice was trembling and his eyes had narrowed to slits. "I think it's just about time . . ."

Gisele made her decision in a matter of split seconds. Weighing the salad and the bowl of soup in each hand she decided on the salad. This she pushed into his face and then stood back fascinated as the messy conglomeration of broken down vegetables and thick mayonnaise blotted out his features.

He clawed the mixture from his eyes cursing in Greek. She stood back and waited until he had clawed most of the contents of the bowl from his eyes then threw the bowl of soup. It was perfectly placed. He screamed profanity as she snatched her dress and handbag from her locker and raced frantically out to St. Catherine Street.

She ran west on the street until she reached Philips Square where she took refuge in the underground comfort station. She paused only to catch her breath.

The comfort station was a gleaming marble room where a trim attendant fussed and polished. Gisele groped in her handbag and found a nickel which she inserted in the toilet doorknob. Soon she was in the cubicle scraping a stray strand of salad from her shoes and adjusting her dishevelled hair.

She returned to St. Catherine Street and watched the crowds hurrying by. "What now?" she asked herself. She dared not return to the restaurant although they owed her a few days' pay. She paused to take stock and soon realized that all she had to show for three days of waiting on tables was a total of $8.45 in tips – most of which was gathered in nickels, dimes and even coppers.

She stopped long enough at the University Street news stand to buy all the evening papers, then walked across the street and entered the department store on the corner. The sight of so much luxury gave her spirits a much-needed lift. She strolled leisurely through the departments gazing enviously at the well-stocked counters.

A display of bathrobes caught her eye. She walked gingerly over to the display and inspected them more closely. They were white towelling and, according to the sign, initials were available at a slight extra charge.

Never had she seen a bathrobe of such startling elegance. Her sense of thrift caused her to inspect the price tag closely. It was priced $6.98 – almost as much as she had earned during her entire stay in Montreal.

"Can I help you, Ma'am?" a small efficient-looking salesgirl stood patiently beside her.

Gisele hesitated for only a moment. "Have you a size 16?"

The salesgirl most certainly had a size 16 and would ma'am care to have initials sewn on the pocket?

Gisele nodded then stood eagerly waiting as the letters "GL" were stitched on the pocket.

Clutching her package tightly she walked west again. Her heels beat a steady tattoo through the bench-lined Dominion Square until she reached Dorchester Street.

Here she slackened her pace and walked leisurely along the crowded street. Her gaze took in the new hotel on her left and the mansion of Victorian type appearance on her right. The latter seemed to lean against each other for support.

The crowd flowing past without giving her a second glance added to her feeling that she was, at last, part of the city. She was, she felt, finally accepted as an individual among a million and a half other individuals. She quickened her pace and ran lightly up the stairs leading to her rooming house.

Once inside her room she ripped the wrappings from her parcel. She carefully withdrew the bath robe and laid it carefully over the end of the bed. Without taking her eyes from it she slipped out of her clothes and wrapped the snowy-white towelling around her.

She fingered the black initials for some time before she leaned wearily on the bed and fell asleep.

It was after seven o'clock when she awakened. The neons were already lighting up the street and the sounds of traffic and voices drifted into the room. She looked at the stack of newspapers she had purchased and thought, with some misgivings, that it was too late to apply for another job that day.

She stared intently at the ceiling and decided that she was lonesome. Very lonesome, she agreed. "Tonight I need company. Perhaps a handsome young man." She smiled to herself.

Showered and dressed she once more went out into the street. Turning west she walked slowly to the corner of Mountain. The street was alive with elaborate signs indicating that night clubs were wide open. "Dance, Dine, Beer, Wine," the letter proclaimed proudly.

She retraced her steps along Dorchester until she neared a cafe which had excited her interest since her first day in the city. A massive sign proclaimed it to be "The Breakers" and a never-ending stream of people continually flowing in and out of its portals.

As she drew opposite the door a taxi pulled up to the curb and a young, smartly dressed girl stepped out. She paused only long enough to hand the driver a bill then, without hesitation, walked into the club.

"But she was unescorted!" Gisele gasped.

She stood staring at the girl's retreating figure then turned and followed.

CHAPTER FIVE

Surprised at her own daring she smiled, with a slight trace of aloofness, at the huge headwaiter whose shoulders were like an ox's and who had a face to match.

"Alone, Miss?" His voice was low to the point where it could easily be described as a growl.

Not trusting her own voice Gisele nodded an affirmative and followed the bulky shoulders into the dining room.

The room was high-ceilinged, discreetly lit and smelled strongly of cigars. Some twenty or thirty people sat around the low tables, in booths or relaxed comfortably in low, yellow lounges.

The walls were painted a deep blue crossed with slanted silver stripes. Framed photographs covered most of the lower level and, from what Gisele could see, were mostly of young men clad in boxing shorts.

No one as much as glanced in her direction as the headwaiter bowed her to a small table set against the wall.

"Having dinner, Miss?" His voice seemed more of a growl than ever.

Confused, and not a little frightened, she nodded negatively.

He looked at her for a long moment. His battered face remained blank but his eyes seemed to harbour the merest hint of a twinkle.

"You'll have a drink, of course."

"Of course." She echoed.

"Sylvain!" He beckoned to a tall, impeccably clad waiter who, almost immediately, came to her table and bowed.

"*Oui, Mam'selle?*"

Frantically she tried to remember what the ladies at the

Auberge ordered. She, herself, had never tasted liquor except for an occasional sip of her father's beer.

"A . . . a . . ." she stammered.

Sylvain's voice, smooth and well-modulated, came to her rescue.

"May I suggest a Cuba Libre, *Mam'selle?*"

"Certainly," she answered striving valiantly to conceal the relief in her voice.

Much to her surprise she did not choke on the first taste. Instead she felt a sense of fine living as she looked at the dark amber contents of her glass with the two crystal clear ice cubes floating near the surface. Rather pleased with herself she let her gaze wander slowly about the room.

At one table four young men, each with his head buried behind a newspaper, sprawled in various positions completely ignoring each other. Two couples, occupying one of the booths, were laughing softly over a table loaded with drinks.

The steady hum of conversation and the obvious fact that the occupants of the cafe were completely at ease, gave Gisele a somewhat sophisticated feeling as if she too, had been coming here for years. She felt perfectly at home.

Suddenly her attention was drawn to two oddly assorted men who entered the club behind Ox Shoulders. While one continued talking the other ordered a drink as if unheeding his companion.

One was a flashily-dressed individual whose neck bulged from behind a collar at least two sizes too small. He wore a loud checkered suit and a vivid yellow tie on which horse shoes, jockey caps and horses heads were painted in bright colors. A diamond stickpin set off the ensemble.

His companion wore a dark grey suit with conservative stripes. His shirt was snowy white and crisp. A black knitted tie was gathered into a small knot and somehow seemed to set off his prematurely grey hair.

Gisele strained her ears in an effort to catch the theme of their conversation. However, the loudly dressed one spiked his speech with too many slangish expressions for her to understand.

Suddenly the grey haired one looked sharply at Gisele. Here eyes swiftly returned to her drink as she tried to fight the blush she felt creeping up her neck and into her cheeks.

From the corner of her eye she saw him motion to Sylvain then hand a card which he took from his wallet.

Sylvain looked briefly in her direction then disappeared into the tiny bar at the end of the room.

Almost immediately a giant of a man emerged holding the card in one hand and with the other, flicking the ashes of from a huge cigar.

Ignoring the two men he stopped at Gisele's table and without saying a word settled his huge frame into the chair facing her.

He thrust his cigar into the left corner of his spacious mouth and looked at her. His eye closed against the rising smoke and she noticed that the eye remaining open was not unkindly. His face was battered . . . but not battered in the way a professional fighter's face is battered. His bore scars of countless brawls. His eyebrows joined over his prominent nose and his jaw jutted out like the bow of a racing sloop.

Gisele sat silent. Her eyes took in his impeccable grooming. His suit was navy blue gabardine. His shirt was crispy-white and a silk navy blue tie was knotted carefully around his neck. He paused to extract a snowy-white linen handkerchief from his breast pocket and wiped his forehead carefully.

The giant was first to speak. "These characters," he jerked his massive head in the direction of the two men, "want to meetcha. You wanna meet these characters?"

"Why . . . I . . ." she stammered in confusion.

"Don't be scair't, Honey. They won't make a pass atcha

– 36 –

or I'll turn 'em down the steps." He pronounced it "Stechs."

Embarrassed but no longer afraid, Gisele answered. "Well, if you think it's all right – although I don't know them I guess . . ."

Without further conversation he reached over and tapped one of the men on the shoulder. "The lady will meetcha." He pushed his chair back but remained seated."

Obviously pleased, the grey-haired one stood, bowed, then introduced himself as Gaston Courtney, proprietor of Le Coq d'Or night club.

Gisele noticed that his left eye twitched. It fascinated her to think that many times, no doubt, the affliction could have been mistaken for a provocative wink.

She sensed that he realized her interest in the twitching eye and turned from it quickly as he indicated his companion. "This is my producer."

"And your name, *Mam'selle* is . . ."

"Gisele Lepine."

The producer broke in vehemently. "I tell you Gassy you're getting soft in the head. This . . ."

The giant removed the cigar from his mouth. "Shaddap," he thundered.

"If I may be so forward," Courtney continued, "may I ask your occupation?"

Bewildered Gisele looked at her newly acquired, giant-sized and self-appointed protector. He smiled back at her through a cloud of cigar smoke. "It's okay, Honey. I'm Jim Schultz. I own this flea trap and you're just as safe here as you are in yah mudda's arms. Safer unless yah mudda's got cauliflower ears."

Gisele managed to return his smile then turned to Courtney. "I'm a waitress."

"And where are you employed, Miss Lepine?"

"Well . . . you see. I left this morning."

"Boss tried to lay you, huh?" Big Jim grinned widely.

Gisele nodded dumbly.

"So." Courtney said pleasantly. "I have a job for you. It may seem rather strange at first, but, I am certain, you will find it far more remunerative than waiting on tables. I will explain."

He ran his hand wearily through his hair before continuing. "I am in need of one girl to fill in with the chorus at my club."

He raised his hands to silence her protest. "I do not care if you are without previous experience. If it were possible I would bring in a girl from New York. As it is I have not sufficient time to do so. It is against my policy to use local girls. You, of course, have not appeared in any chorus here therefore I do not consider you in that category. Will you accept the position?"

"She'll take it." Big Jim answered the question.

"Very well," Courtney replied. He rose and bowed once more at Gisele. "*A bientot*," he said politely and without a backward glance left the club.

His companion also rose and turned to her. "Rehearsal tomorrow. Three o'clock. Bring rehearsal clothes. I said three o'clock." He turned and hurried after Courtney.

CHAPTER SIX

Gisele was frantic as she watched them disappear from the room. She turned to Schultz. "But *m'sieu* . . ."

"What are you worrying about, Honey?" His eyes twinkling with amusement. "One of the chorus broads is knocked up and he needs a new one. You're the new one. Simple ain't it?"

His calmness didn't dispel her fears. "But I have never even been inside a night club. What . . . how . . ."

He waved her to silence. "Soon fix that." He turned in his chair and called to one of the four men huddled behind newspapers. "Hey Shakespeare."

The man lowered his paper just enough to peer over the top. "What do you want? Pig!"

"C'mere."

The man slowly folded the newspaper, carefully set it down on the table and drank a gulp of beer before moving. When he stood up Gisele noticed he was young and well built. His suit seemed to have been poured on him, his shoes gleamed and his shirt looked laundry fresh.

She guessed he was about 26. His hair was as black as her own and, as he drew nearer, she noticed faint lines of dissipation on his handsome face.

He looked insolently at Schultz. "What do you want? Pig!"

Jim ignored the reference. "What time you gonna make your rounds?"

The young man glanced at his watch and replied. "In about ten minutes."

Schultz waved a fat hand in Gisele's direction. "Here's company."

The young man glanced at her for the first time and drew up a chair. He smiled as Jim rose to leave. "Get going, Pig," he said.

Jim looked seriously at Gisele. "Don't let this junior grade wolf make any passes at you, Baby."

Gisele laughed and turned to her new companion. "Why do you call *M'sieu* Schultz . . . Pig?"

"For the same reason he calls me Shakespeare. The title fits." He said seriously. Then he smiled and said. "My name's Jimmy Holden. I'm on *The Chronicle*. What's your name?"

"Gisele Lepine." She liked the way he shook her hand.

"Well Gisele, I have to do a show at El Zebra first. Do you mind?"

"I would love to go." Her enthusiasm knew no bounds as he led her from the cafe.

As Jimmy signalled for a taxi Gisele noticed he was freshly barbered. The way he wore his clothes fascinated her. He was, she decided, almost fanatically fanatic about his appearance.

She didn't know that Jimmy Holden was the fashion plate in the industry whose members were usually depicted as being one step removed above the average freight hopper. Holden, however would rather buy clothes than eat – and frequently did.

In the excitement of the meeting Gisele completely forgot that his was her first taxi ride. She settled herself comfortably against the cushions and looked with interest at Jimmy.

"Taking stock?" He asked the question suddenly.

She turned her eyes quickly to the front. "You were very kind to take me with you."

She wondered if he heard her as he was paying little or no attention to what she was saying. He grasped her hand and leaned forward eagerly in the cab. "Look," he almost shouted, "Peel and Ste. Kit's. Beautiful sight – isn't it?"

She looked out the window at the multi-colored lights blinking on and off. The intersection was crowded with jostling people. "It's like New Year's Eve," she said.

As they passed the street she turned to Jimmy. "You like Montreal don't you Jimmy?"

"Like it? Like it? I'm madly in love with it. I was born here. Over in the East End. When was a kid I used to walk all the way from Delorimier Avenue to Peel and St. Catherine – just to look at the city."

He was still holding her hand when the cab turned north and stopped before the elaborate entrance to El Zebra.

A uniformed doorman stalked majestically to the cab and, with deft movements, opened the door. Bowing to Gisele he said, "*Bonsoir, Mam'selle.*" Jimmy paid off the driver, handed a coin to the doorman and followed her up the stairs.

By this time she was perfectly at ease with Jimmy. Even the splendor of El Zebra's palatial lounge did not cause her the slightest discomfort. She gazed with interest at the padded leather walls and the spacious lounge which led from the alcove on their right.

A Latin type headwaiter bowed her to a ringside table and, at the same time, chatted amiably with Jimmy. Jimmy she noticed, was very well known in the club. Parties at almost every table called greetings to him as they passed.

They eventually got settled and Jimmy ordered a Cuba Libre for her. She liked the thought that he noticed what she had been drinking at The Breakers. She didn't hear him order a drink for himself but the waiter re-appeared with her drink plus a bottle of beer for Jimmy.

She looked puzzled for a moment. Jimmy laughed.

"I drink only lager beer. 'Last Longer on Lager' is my motto. Got so I don't even have to order it anymore, they just bring it."

Smiling politely she reached across the table and touched his hand. "Jimmy, you have not asked me where I come from or what I do, or what I was doing alone in The Breakers. Is it that you are not interested?"

He leaned his elbows on the table and stared at her seriously. "Sugar Puss, if you want me to know anything about yourself you will tell me without me having to ask. Big Jim said to bring you along on my rounds for some reason or other. 'Why?' is immaterial."

"The fact that Schultz asked me to escort you stamps you as being a good kid. He doesn't allow tramps in his spot and the fact that I'm with you tonight practically assures you of being safe from a fast pass. Jim's a pretty good guy and someday I'm going to call him something else besides Pig."

She found herself growing fond of this strange young man. There was something bothering her, however and it was only natural that she should ask him. She couldn't very well ask anyone else, she reasoned. Embarrassed she leaned over the table and, in a low voice, asked. What are 'rehearsal clothes,' Jimmy?"

He was half turned in his seat trying to attract a waiter and answered over his shoulder. "They're the doo-dads chorus dolls wear when they rehearse."

Her next question caught him off guard and he paused with his glass in mid-air.

"Where can I buy some?"

"What in hell's name do you want with rehearsal clothes, Sugar Puss?" He sounded awe-struck and was.

"I . . . I start at Le Coq d'Or tomorrow and was told to bring them."

A smile split his face. "Have you ever danced professionally before?"

She lowered her eyes. "No."

"Well, Sugar Puss, you're a surprising person. Here's

what you do. Go out tomorrow and buy yourself a pair of comfortable loafers and bring them to a shoe repair store. Get rubber soles glued on them. Then," he scribbled a Burnside Street address on a scrap of paper, "take this over to my friend at this address – name is Brownie – and he'll give you everything else you need. Then get a small traveling bag and . . . *voila!* . . . you're a chorus girl. Almost."

An ear shattering fanfare drowned out her mumbled thanks and she turned to see ten young girls dance out from the wings. All were young and fresh looking. They danced their way through an intricate routine. Gisele thought it was the most beautiful spectacle she had ever witnessed.

She found herself trying to compare it with the St. Jean Baptiste parade and found it impossible – and not a little sacrilegious at that.

Jimmy was looking at the show with what seemed a great deal of indifference.

She was going to speak with him but saw he was scribbling notes on the back of a numbered place card. He seemed a little bored so she remained silent throughout the entire show. The orchestra leader was introduced and applauded. He then raised his baton and the band resumed its dance music.

"Like the show?"

"It was beautiful, Jimmy."

"Stinks," was his only comment as he grasped her elbow tightly and steered her into the lounge.

CHAPTER SEVEN

The lounge was crowded when they entered. Several stopped to talk to Jimmy as they stood at the bar. He didn't bother to introduce her to anyone . . . she wondered why.

When at last they were alone and able to speak he asked her how long she had known Courtney.

"About ten minutes longer than I have known you, Jimmy. I met him for the first time tonight."

"Don't get too involved with that twitch-face louse, Sugar Puss."

"Why Jimmy?"

"He's a . . . aw t'hell with it. You tired?"

"Not really."

"Good. Let's go wake up Sammy."

As he helped her down the stairs of the club she felt like Cinderella, the girl in the English story who had to return home before midnight.

They were settled in a cab when Gisele asked.

"Who is Sammy?"

"That's the slightly insane person I live with. We share an apartment over on Shuter Street. He works on the paper too. Someone once accused him of having brains and he is still trying to disprove the allegation."

Waking Sammy proved no problem whatsoever. In fact Sammy was quite wide awake. As they entered the tiny apartment he was standing, glass in hand, making a lengthy speech dealing with the abject futility of a goldfish's existence.

He waved to them then came over. He was short and unbelievably thin. A pair of huge horn-rimmed glasses set off his flaming red hair. He noticed her gazing at his skinny frame. "Strictly a waste of skin, ain't I honey?"

She extended her hand which he shook vigorously. "I've been waiting to meet you for years. But years, my deah. By the way – what's your name?"

"Gisele."

He took her by the arm and introduced her to the dozen-odd people who jampacked the main room of the place. She had never seen such a widely assorted group of before. A retired boxing champ with a flattened nose; a professional gambler; a girl elevator operator from the Sherbrooke Street Hotel; a singing comedian from a Stanley Street night club; and an acrobatic dancer who was appearing on the same bill.

The air was blue with smoke. The party was noisy in a casual way and everyone seemed to know everyone else.

A balding young man approached her and asked if she could rumba. He promised to teach her but said they wouldn't be able to hear the music over the noise of the crowd. "And you can get arrested for doing a rumba without music," he added.

Gisele learned later that he was the leader of the most famous orchestra in the city. She also learned that he had a pet skunk and was peeved because he couldn't bring it on the band stand with him.

It was well after five in the morning when Jimmy offered to take Gisele home. The party had subdued considerably. Several guests had fallen fast asleep on the floor. Sammy and the acrobatic dancer were in the kitchen drinking rye.

Gisele stopped Jimmy in the act of flagging a taxi. "Please don't. It's such a lovely night. Or should I say morning? Let's walk."

"Inexpensive too." Jimmy smiled and held her firmly by the arm.

They turned west on Sherbrooke and walked silently past McGill University grounds. By looking down the side streets Gisele could see the tops of the tall buildings immediately south. The sun danced on the upper-most windows on the higher ones and deep shadows fell across Sherbrooke Street.

They turned down Stanley Street where Jimmy stopped long enough to feed a lump of sugar to an aged dairy horse. "Hi'yah, Sugar Puss," he said stroking its mane.

They paused at the door of her room. Gisele wondered what Jimmy would do. She also wondered what she would do if he did.

She didn't wonder long, however. At the entrance to her rooming house he shook her hand and said a soft 'good night'. She watched him turn and descend the stairs, his steps barely making a sound.

She entered her room and quickly ran to the window just in time to see him hail a cab going east on Dorchester and disappear from view.

She undressed slowly and relaxed on the bed. "Can it be," she thought, "that I have fallen in love with almost the first man I have met in the city?"

She wished now that Jimmy had come into the room. True, she expected, that he would treat her with nothing but respect. Then again she wondered if she actually wanted him to treat her so. She debated in her mind whether or not she would have allowed him to make love to her.

Then, deciding that life was all very confusing, she fell asleep.

It seemed as if she had just closed her eyes when there was a loud knocking on the door.

Startled, she sat up. "Who is it?"

"Shakespeare." Jimmy's voice came loudly through the door.

Breathing a prayer of thanks for her new bathrobe she quickly drew it around her and opened the door to find Jimmy leaning nonchalantly against the wall.

He held a large paper bag before his eyes. "Look Sugar Puss – breakfast. Am I invited?"

They sat side by side on the bed using a chair for a table and ate toasted cream cheese sandwiches and drank steaming coffee from two large containers.

It was noon before Jimmy suggested they go shopping for rehearsal clothes. He seemed to know his way around the department stores and Gisele heard several sales girls call him by name. She thought it was foolish for her to be jealous of this fact.

By 2:30 he had managed to gather a complete set of everything she needed to launch her career as a lady of the chorus. He dropped her off at the Coq d'Or with a warning. "Now, Sugar Puss, don't get nervous. Just do everything you are told the best way you can. The dance director is a mad Russian wench but she's a good sport. I have already phoned her and she promised to take good care of you."

Gisele listened attentively to what he had to say and promised to call him after rehearsal. She was surprised to find herself merely curious – not frightened – just curious. She finally decided it was Jimmy's personality that had made her so.

She walked through the lobby into one of the most dismal of all sights – a night club in the afternoon. Chairs were stacked on tables and a melancholy air hung over the room. It was a much larger club than El Zebra, she noticed. A balcony ran around the entire place and a huge dance floor was installed at one end, raised quite high from the floor.

Three girls leaned against the bar at one end of the room. They were smoking and drinking cokes as Gisele approached. "You the new girl?" one asked.

"Yes. My name is Gisele."

"Where you out of?" another asked curiously.

"Where am I what," she answered puzzled.

The girl who first spoke to her smiled. "She means where are you from?"

"Oh. I come from northern Quebec. A small village . . .

you have probably never heard of it."

The third girl exploded from her bar stool. "Up north? Man – wotta jernt. Was up in Ste. Agathe last week-end. Man – wotta time I had."

They all laughed.

One with reddish brown hair looked serious. "Say. You're local. Didn't know the joint used local girls."

Gisele explained she had never danced in a chorus before.

They didn't seem overly surprised at the confession. "You'll still be the only local in the line."

Gisele asked what a 'line' was. The girls explained it was a professional name for a chorus.

"I'm afraid I have much to learn." She admitted.

"Don't let it get you down Baby," one said. "At least you won't have any immigration headaches – you're the only Canuck among us."

Soon the rest of the girls arrived. Most were dressed in slacks of brilliant colors and short jackets. All wore bandannas around their hair and sun glasses – and all looked conspicuous.

After being introduced to each one in turn Gisele sat listening to their conversation. Most of it, she discovered, concerned last nights' dates.

"So we went out on the Strip and had ourselves a swim but on the way back he said . . ."

"Did I know he was going to bring me down to that East End dive where all the broken down old bags were . . ."

"And so I told him, I said. If you think for minute . . ."

The chatter continued until a fierce looking woman entered in a solemn parade of one. One of the girls whispered softly. "Look, the old hag can walk four abreast and still be alone."

She stood before the girls glaring. "Well?" Her voice echoed through the club.

Without a word they headed for the far end of the room where a stairway led down to their dressing quarters.

"That," one girl breathed to Gisele, "is Madame Chechovska. Don't let her scare you. She tries to make you think she's a proper bitch but we know she's really a doll."

Gisele's introduction to the mysteries of precision dancing was the subject of conversation for all of four minutes.

When they stopped for a breather the girl with the reddish brown hair brought over two cokes. She handed one to Gisele. "You're doing slightly terrific Kid – you know it?"

"Thank you." Was all Gisele could manage.

The girl slouched against the bar beside her. "My name's Trixie. Helluva name that. Pop said he named me after a mongrel that died but Ma said it was a burlesque broad he used to sleep with."

Gisele wondered whether or not to laugh when Madame called them back to the floor for a final run through the routines.

After dismissal the girls dashed for the dressing room. A bus boy in shirt sleeves knocked politely on the door and handed Trixie a note. She read it.

"Look kids. A message from Garcia. The wolves are upstairs and we're all invited to The Breakers for several fast beers. Transportation too."

The girls began to dress hurriedly and soon scrambled up the stairs en masse.

Several young men were standing at the bar drinking when they arrived. Trixie screamed, "There's my lover man," and threw herself into the arms of a stout individual with thinning hair whose face seemed to be creased into a perpetual smile.

They all left the club together and piled into a fleet of parked cars. Gisele followed Trixie into a long blue convertible owned by the fat one. Trixie was shouting, "Let me drive, let me drive." She was already behind the wheel and expertly steered the car into the west-bound traffic.

The cavalcade proceeded noisily along Dorchester Street causing heads to turn and not a few passing cars to veer quickly to the curb.

At The Breakers the gang whooped and hollered as they stormed into the cafe. Gisele felt someone touch her arm and turned to face Diane, the only platinum blonde in the chorus.

"You haven't been around much, have you Gisele?"

"I . . . I guess not." She was surprised to hear herself called anything but 'Kid,' 'Honey' or 'Baby.'

"I'm captain of the line. I have to tell you that so you will know who to come to for your day off and other things. Incidentally, the name is Diane."

They found a table and ordered beer before Gisele excused herself and went to the lobby telephone to call Jimmy.

He sounded pleased to hear her although she wondered how he possibly could over the noise of *The Chronicle* office. He promised to "grab a cab" and come to The Breakers on the double.

CHAPTER EIGHT

Much to the delight of the few customers who happened to be in The Breakers the girls overran the spot. Two went through an impromptu song and dance they used to perform as a sister team on the night club circuit.

Gisele noticed Big Jim sitting at a table before the bar playing gin rummy with a dark young man. She fought back a desire to run over and thank him for his kindness of the previous night.

Eventually he looked up from his cards and nodded to her. "How yah doin', Honey?"

"Very good, *M'sieu* Schultz."

Within ten minutes Jimmy arrived with Sammy. Sammy appeared more than a little tight. He walked slowly and precisely to Diane, held her chin between his thumb and fore finger and gravely announced. "I gaze upon you and find you fair."

Leaving Diane he repeated the process with Gisele. "You too," he said happily and settled at the table.

Jimmy held Gisele's hand but Sammy held the floor. He beseeched Diane to join his movement to restore the democratic rights of the Australian Kiwi. "The way they are prevented from voting is a stinking crime," he announced to all within earshot.

Sammy downed a double rye in record time then spoke to Diane again.

He pulled his chair closer to the table and Jimmy moved closer to Gisele. Their knees touched and a pleasant feeling ran through her. She looked at him cautiously as he talked to Sammy. His good grooming still fascinated her as she appraised an immaculate light grey suit.

Meanwhile Sammy's voice continued on a multitude of subjects. Diane, she saw, was apparently attracted to the amazing character Jimmy had described as being "slightly insane."

Diane nodded in agreement as Sammy proposed to set up a fund with which to build a night club in the editorial department of *The Chronicle*. The bar would run beside Sammy's desk and the floor show would be held where the managing editor's office was at present. He proposed to open the club three days after the City of Toronto was given a decent burial. The three days, he explained, was out of respect.

Jimmy silenced Sammy long enough to ask Diane what time she had to return to the club for the first show.

"This is my night off," she answered.

"So then," Jimmy said, "how about us all going down to the East End?"

The four piled into the rear seat of a cab with Diane sitting on Sammy's lap and insisting their positions be reversed.

Gisele was crowded close against Jimmy and liked it. His arm was around her shoulders in a protective gesture. She wondered what Montreal would be like if she had not met him. Suppose, she thought, he tired of her? The idea frightened her.

She snuggled closer as the cab sped east on Dorchester through narrow streets lined with tired-looking slum houses. They finally turned north to St. Catherine Street and stopped outside a three-storey building in front of which, by means of a massive sign – proclaimed it to be "The Spaghetti Palace."

"Quite a spot this," Sammy stated as they climbed the long flight of stairs. "It averages three guns to a table."

As they entered the room they were greeted enthusiastically by the owner who personally escorted them to a table. He sent over a bottle of Chablis with the compliments of the house and briskly ordered his waiters to their table.

"That guy's still afraid of you, Palsy," Sammy whispered grimly to Jimmy.

"So?" Jimmy said before busying himself with a menu. Gisele shivered with a thrill of fascination at several sinister types who stared coldly at Jimmy. There was a tenseness in the air and she wished he had chosen some other place to have dinner.

Most of the women were over-painted and wore dresses which she hadn't seen in the West End. They were loose types of persons, she decided. And their male companions had an air of toughness about them that made her uncomfortable. Some had scars on their faces and one particular couple nodded toward Jimmy and conversed in low tones. She wished they were all back at The Breakers.

Later she was to learn that Jimmy was as feared in the district as any policeman. He had once written a series of articles on the dope trade at Clarke and St. Catherine corner which resulted in many arrests – although the leader escaped.

The stories had not endeared him to the demi-mode which frequented the district and at one time a West End gambler had offered even money that Jimmy would wind up in a cement overcoat at the bottom of Lachine Canal if he ventured into the district before the affair cooled off.

But Jimmy came and went in the district and remained unscathed. Some claimed he was just lucky. Others said the fact that he was from the East End himself made him immune to retribution. Those in the know explained patiently that Jimmy and Luigi had grown up together and had been fast friends all their lives. That fact, they said was the real reason Jimmy Holden was still walking around. If prompted they would further explain that Luigi controlled the muscle in the city. He was a gambler and a big one. His boys were feared the length and breadth of the Island and it wasn't considered wise to push around any of his friends.

Whatever the reason Jimmy himself was the least concerned. He felt more at home on the east side of Bleury Street and often thought about his neighborhood gang, most especially after a lengthy session of lager beer. He was one of the few, he mused, who had remained out of jail.

The foursome ate in a silence broken only by a single remark from Sammy who declared that no man is ever lonesome while eating spaghetti. "Keeps him too busy," he explained.

They sat around drinking wine for some time before Sammy rose. "I leave to write my deathless prose. I also leave you to the check." Bowing he took Diane's arm and they both left the restaurant.

As soon as they were alone Jimmy held Gisele's hand in both of his. "I'm getting very fond of you, Sugar Puss. Do you mind?"

They sat in silence for a few minutes then finished the wine.

He called for the check and was told it was on the house. He slipped the waiter a bill and they left the restaurant.

They stood outside the place for a while as Jimmy looked at the passers-by. "Same old faces," he murmured and, holding her arm, walked toward St. Lawrence Main.

"How would you like to come up to the apartment for a drink and some record playing?" He asked.

She didn't trust herself to answer. Instead she shook her head in an affirmative gesture avoiding his eyes. She wondered if the visit to the apartment would be confined to playing records. She found herself hoping it wouldn't be.

The cab ride to Shuter Street was made in silence. They mounted the stairs and Jimmy switched on the lights.

"I'm rather weary of asking guests to excuse the untidiness of the place – so I won't."

She looked about the apartment which was in a wild

state of disorder. The curtain rod in the doorway between the two rooms was being used to hang suits. About six of them replaced the non-existent curtain forcing anyone to stoop low when passing between the two rooms.

The single clothes closet was massive – but not massive enough. The racks were packed solidly with suits like a tailor's stock room. Others hung from behind doors and one from an overhead pipe in the tiny kitchen.

Shoes littered the floor and countless ties were draped over the doorknobs and whatever other obstacle protruded sufficiently to accommodate them. Two typewriters were almost buried under an avalanche of books, newspapers and magazines. Ashtrays were filled to overflowing and cellophane wrappers from laundered shirts were everywhere.

Jimmy disappeared into the kitchen and emerged, after much splashing, with two clean glasses and a bottle of beer. Placing the beer on the coffee table, after pushing several books to the floor, he grinned at her. "This is for me Sugar Puss, what's for you?"

"I think I'll have a beer too . . . a lager beer."

Both reached for the bottle at the same time. Their bodies touched and Gisele felt a warm glow spreading inside her. She felt Jimmy's arm encircle her waist and his free hand turn her upwards. Lips parted, she yielded to the kiss, running her hand through his black hair as she pressed herself against him.

After an eternity they parted breathlessly. Jimmy looked deep into her eyes.

"Hello Sugar Puss."

He went to the record player and riffled through the records stacked on its top. A piano solo of "Clair de Lune" filled the room.

They drank in silence as the record ended and the automatic changer replayed it once more.

Neither seemed to notice.

The buzzing of the telephone broke the spell.

Jimmy cursed softly and reached under the bed for the instrument. His hand emerged holding the headpiece. He smiled at Gisele. "Always keep the damn thing there so we won't trip over it."

It was Sammy.

His voice sounded more slurred than usual. "This is Samuel Hoffman, internationally known chess wizard and raconteur – whatever in hell that means – telling you I won't be home this enchanted evening."

"I couldn't care less," Jimmy said and hung up.

He turned on a small blue lamp which balanced precariously atop the debris on the cluttered desk then extinguished the rest of the lights.

They held each other in close embrace for some time. "There's a bathrobe of Sammy's in the showers," he said evenly as Gisele arose.

Without a word she entered the bathroom and soon Jimmy heard the shower splashing. He donned his own robe and sat smoking until she re-entered the room carrying her clothes over her arm.

Sammy's bathrobe felt tight across her shoulders. The front, where its lapels tucked one under the other, was not large enough to conceal Gisele's breasts. She pulled hard on the sash only to have the robe bulge at the top and reveal a bare expanse to her waist like a plunging neck-line.

Jimmy's eyes froze on the cleavage as she fussed with the robe. He rose and walked to her in silence. She stood, fearful in part – hopeful in part, and accepted his embrace. He kissed her lightly on the forehead and continued on into the shower.

As soon as she heard him splashing about behind the door she walked into the kitchen and reached into the lower shelf of the fridge to get a bottle of beer. Stooping low the bathrobe hampered her movements and, for a moment, she was certain it would rip if she flexed her shoulder muscles.

She brought the bottle to the coffee table and reached for the opener only to have the fabric of the robe hinder her movement. In desperation she threw it off and stood nude – and comfortable.

Thus Jimmy found her as he came out of the shower drying himself briskly with a heavy towel. He stood for an interminable moment looking at her then, shedding his own robe, sat on the side of the bed and accepted the glass she offered.

He looked at her hungrily over the glass as he drank. Her ebony-black hair fell to a point just below her shoulders and the soft glow of the light played upon it to form a hazy halo when she was between him and the lamp. Her thin skin was dark. Like the color of coffee with too much cream, he thought. There were no white patches where a bathing suit had obstructed they rays of the sun. He wondered about this.

She sat beside him, his leg pressing close to his. She said nothing. The tall glass in her hand was gathering a mist on the outside and she erased it with her fingers. Suddenly she turned to him.

"Are you happy, *Bebé*?" She spoke in French.

"*Oui ma cherie*," he answered.

She sighed lazily and placed her glass on the table. He watched her as she stretched out on the bed. So much like a cat, he thought.

He turned slightly and looked down at her. The lamp cast a bluish glow across her flat stomach. It was like television, he thought. Her breasts were almost hidden in the shadow his body threw across her. He didn't trust himself to speak. Instead he drank slowly looking steadily into the light until his eyes were blurred.

She whimpered like a spaniel. "Please Jimmy."

He rose and went into the shower. She could hear the water running as he splashed cold water on his face. He didn't bother to dry himself before returning.

Breathlessly she waited until she felt the bed sag as he settled his weight upon it. Then she was in his arms. Her fingernails dug themselves into his back and her lips bruised his as she fought her inner emotions.

He gathered her in his arms once more and kissed her cruelly. She slid her hand to his neck and pressed his face to hers.

Her slight gasp of pain could not be heard above the lilting strains of "Clair de Lune" as the record player played it for the twelfth time.

CHAPTER NINE

The telephone rang insistently beneath the bed. Gisele stirred lazily then awoke with a start. She groped in the darkness conscious that she was alone and not a little frightened at the thought.

When she finally answered her voice was scarcely above a whisper.

It was Jimmy. "Good morning Sugar Puss. There's a fresh bottle of cream in the fridge and some coffee somewhere in the kitchen."

She wanted to ask him about last night but couldn't raise sufficient courage before he hung up. His voice, however, dispelled a sense of shame she had felt since the telephone roused her.

Feeling her way through the darkness she found the bathroom light switch. The sudden glare of light hurt her eyes and she felt stuffed and heavy headed. She ran cold water over her hands and splashed her face.

A glance in the mirror told her she still looked the same regardless of how different she felt.

"Today, Gisele," she told herself, "you are a woman." She paused for some time reliving every one of the precious moments of the night. "You are," she said, "a young woman in love – and what's more you look it."

After a fast shower she wrapped Sammy's bathrobe around herself and, after hunting through the littered kitchen, found the coffee. She brewed herself a strong mixture then returned to the bed and drank the entire contents of the glass percolator.

It was close to ten o'clock when the idea struck her. She pulled aside the heavy drapes and let what little sunshine could find its way through the grimy pane into the room.

Under the pitiless glare of the sun the apartment looked more dismal than ever. With an effort she managed to open the window to let some much-needed fresh air into the rooms. Then, hunting through the closet, found a pair of Sammy's slacks and an ancient tattered sweatshirt.

With a tea towel wrapped around her hair she looked typical of the countless thousands of Montreal housewives busily engaged in the never-ending battle with dirt. In her case, however, it was no mere battle – it was all-out warfare.

Under a camel hair coat, thrown carelessly over the day couch, she discovered an unopened parcel of laundry. No finder of buried treasure could have seized upon it with more delight.

Placing it to one side she turned her efforts to the kitchen. Soon a large collection of liquor bottles, tin cans, broken glasses and bread crusts were thrown down the incinerator followed closely by the contents of some half dozen trays.

Books were separated from magazines and old socks, and stacked neatly on shelves. Two typewriters were replaced in their cases and floors were swept, windows were washed, laundry was collected and wrapped, and linen was changed.

It was almost three in the afternoon before the apartment reached a condition which met with her approval. She sat down heavily and looked about for a corner that may have escaped her attention.

After a short breathing space she showered, dressed then brewed another pot of coffee.

She heard a key being fitted in the lock and Sammy's toneless whistling. He walked breezily into the apartment throwing his hat on the day couch. Suddenly he stopped, looked around and said. "So sorry, wrong apartment."

He turned as if to go then spied Gisele calmly drinking coffee.

Turning around and surveying the rooms from all angles he said seriously, "Who in hell let the fresh air in here?"

Gisele rose silently and removed his hat from the day couch placing it on the hat rack from which some two dozen neckties had been removed. "Want some coffee, Sammy?"

"Coffee hell. I need a drink."

He walked rapidly into the kitchen, stopped in his tracks and screamed. "Oh no! Not that!"

He came out with a bottle of rye and two glasses. He held the glasses up to the light. "First time in two years we've had clean glasses. Remarkable, really."

He poured her a generous shot of rye then sat beside her on the bed. They drank silently for some time then Gisele made more coffee and sandwiches.

"Sammy."

"Uh-huh," he replied without looking at her.

"You have known Jimmy for some time; have you not?"

"Uh-huh."

"Does he have a . . . regular girlfriend?"

"Uh-huh."

A sudden fear swept over her as she asked. "Who?"

"You."

She watched Sammy debate whether to take a drink of coffee or of rye. Rye won the decision.

Eagerly she attempted to find out more about Jimmy. After all he was her lover – her first, in fact. No one had better right to know about him than her. Jimmy spoke very little about himself.

"You're his best friend? Aren't you Sammy?"

"Not quite, princess. You see I only moved in here with Jimmy after Bill Tyler left town. He was on the paper too and between him and Jimmy the town wasn't safe. They used to tear it apart every night."

"Where is this Bill now?"

"Don't know exactly. Last time I heard from him he was in Miami getting rid of a lot of illusions he had about the newspaper business in Montreal."

The door opened and Jimmy entered carrying a tailor's box. "Momma Mia," he said with surprise as he looked around.

"I'm the only piece of garbage that wasn't thrown out," Sammy commented.

Jimmy opened the box and took out a light sharkskin suit. He placed it on a hanger and, holding it at arm's length, looked at it in admiration.

Gisele interrupted his reverie. "We were talking about Bill Tyler."

Jimmy's face brightened immediately. "Got a letter from him this morning."

"Where's he at?" Sammy's voice was getting thick.

"Still in Miami. He wanted to know if we still had to kiss fannies to keep jobs up here."

"What's he doing?"

"God knows. All he said was that he was 'living' – but he was always saying that anyway."

Jimmy brought himself a cup from the kitchen and poured himself some coffee. "*C'est la vie, eh Bebe?*" He put his arm around her fondly.

She responded tenderly to his kiss then said, "It's opening night tonight, darling, and I had better go home and change." She pronounced it 'shay-ng'.

Jimmy smiled. It was the first time her French accent had crept into her speech. It was fascinating, and he told her so.

Sammy stood up, his hands waving. "Tonight a bright new star is born. We give you for the first time on any stage – Gisele Lepine." He bowed too low and stumbled.

He placed his hat on the back of his head, finished his drink at a gulp and left.

As soon as the door closed they were in each other's

arms. "Jimmy," she whispered, "last night . . . it was the first time. I . . ."

"That wasn't hard to figure out, Sugar Puss."

CHAPTER TEN

Gisele was first to arrive at the Coq d'Or. It was fully an hour before the scheduled time of the show, but already the club was jammed with a near-capacity crowd.

She made her way to the dressing room and sat nervously checking on her wardrobe. Diane arrived some twenty minutes later dressed in slacks and wearing a pair of sun glasses.

She took the glasses off and held them up for Gisele's inspection. "Sammy gave them to me last night. Cute huh?" She began to undress slowly. "That guy Sammy. What a character. We wound up this morning in the filthiest dive you ever did see. Imagine me walking along the waterfront at 5:30 in the morning?"

Gisele smiled. "I saw Sammy this afternoon. He'll probably be in with Jimmy for the last show.

Diane threw back her head letting her platinum locks cascade down her back. "I sure hope so. Sammy has something. I don't know what it is – but he's got something. Can't be money. He borrowed car fare from me to bring me home this morning." She leaned back in the chair, sighed deeply and murmured, "Wotta man."

Gisele fussed with the gown she was to wear in the first number. It was a lengthy white dress cut low at the neck and trimmed with lace. The routine was set to a Strauss waltz and she liked the dance better than the other two which they would do during the hour-long show.

The other girls began to arrive singly and in pairs. They took their places at the dressing table and applied the heavy makeup needed under the brilliant lights. The conversation centered, as usual, about their respective dates of the previous evening.

Diane, sitting nearest the door, cut short Trixie's description of a tour through Chinatown as the muffled tones of the fanfare drifted down the stairs. "This is it, kids." She stood up and led the girls up to the stage.

Gisele, standing on Diane's left, waited nervously behind the heavy curtain which separated them from the customers. She heard the master of ceremonies announcing them in front of the curtain and applause swell up from the crowded club.

As the curtains parted her nervousness suddenly left her and she picked up the step with ease. She swore she would be ever grateful to Madame Chechovska for her expert tuition.

The number ended and Gisele joined the rush down stairs to the dressing room. They had to change fast and most of the girls were gasping for breath after the energetic opening number.

Trixie struggled out of her costume and nodded her head at Gisele. "Did you get this kid?" She asked. "First show and she's hoofing like a veteran. Makes the rest of us old bags look sick."

Gisele was pleased with her performance and thankful that Trixie had noticed it. She liked dancing and was rather proud she had managed to do the entire number without a single misstep.

The second and third numbers went off without mishap and Gisele found herself looking forward to the next show. This was her life, she decided. She wondered how long a chorus girl could work before she found herself too old to stand the rigors of constant rehearsals and daily shows.

The girls were changing into street clothes when the bus boys began to arrive with notes. Then handed them all to Diane who relayed the messages.

"Trixie, Phil wants you to bring a gal and meet him at Roland's table . . ."

"Eve, some jerk from Rochester wants to know if you ever worked the Cockeyed Goose in Buffalo. If so, he says, come up for a drink. If not, come up anyway – he sounds like a wandering wolf . . ."

"Gisele. Jimmy Holden is in with Sammy. He says congratulations and come up for a fast beer between shows."

The girls were suddenly quiet. Eve turned to Gisele. "You know Holden?"

"Yes."

Eve's young-old face took on a surprised expression. She turned and looked at the girls. "How do you like that? Her first day as a hoofer and already God Almighty Jimmy Holden is dating her."

Gisele wanted to say that she was his woman, but instead said, "We're friends."

She was blushing furiously as she followed Diane out of the room.

Finding Jimmy's table in the crowded club was easy. Harry, an old timer in the ranks of the city's waiters, formed a one-man flying wedge through the crowd.

She sat beside Jimmy and asked anxiously. "Did I look all right? I was nervous at first but not when I started dancing. Did I look too different from the rest?"

He stopped her abruptly. "You'll do, Sugar Puss."

Sammy was enthusiastic. He came around the table to kiss her forehead. "Gisele *ma petite bebe* you are the greatest thing to hit show business here since Fifi D'Orsay. You are superb, magnificent, you are – shall we say – *tres, tres*? A combination of Pavlowa and *Mam'selle* St. Cyr. You were great."

He returned to his seat fumbling in his shirt pocket from where he drew a wilted daisy. Bowing to Diane he handed the dilapidated plant to her.

"To you," he said in a deep voice. "A small token to express my profound love. I hope you will treasure it in the happy years to come. Oh Babe."

Diane accepted the drooping flower and fastened it in her hair. The thing hung lazily over one eye and people at surrounding tables wondered if the party was getting a bit too stiff.

Sammy was delighted. "To me fair friend, you never shall grow old." He was about to continue the sonnet when Diane protested.

"Don't give me Shakespeare. I want something original like you told me this morning on the waterfront."

Jimmy looked sharply at Sammy who squirmed uncomfortably.

"You write poetry?"

Sammy nodded sadly. "You'll keep my secret, won't you pal?"

A waiter rescued Sammy by bringing a note for Gisele.

Surprised she read: "Come to the office immediately." It was signed "Gaston Courtney."

She turned to the party. "It's from Mister Courtney. Maybe he did not like my dancing so well. I had better go."

Jimmy grasped her arm as she rose. "Be careful of that no-good bastard." She saw a hint of anger in his eyes.

A bull-necked individual opened the door at her knock and held it open as she crossed the huge office to the highly polished mahogany desk behind which Courtney sat.

He greeted her with courtesy. "Drink?" She declined politely and sat down.

Suddenly she wished she had removed her heavy stage make-up before coming upstairs.

"You were surprisingly talented tonight Miss Lepine." His voice gave no hint that he was either pleased or angry.

She managed a small "Thank you."

"I think you will find working for me a pleasure."

"I am certain of that Monsieur Courtney."

He rose and circled the desk. Taking one of her hands he said softly. "Sometimes, my dear, when one is new in the theatrical business one finds one's self attracted to the wrong type of person. Among people we regard as wrong types are scandal mongers. You understand, of course?"

She nodded.

He dropped her hand and said, "That will be all Miss Lepine."

She hurried from the office.

CHAPTER ELEVEN

At the table Jimmy, Sammy and Diane were in the midst of a vigorous discussion about the new chorus routines. They didn't question her regarding her visit to Courtney's office and she didn't volunteer any information.

The boys waited until the second and final show had ended then, on Jimmy's suggestion, headed for a rough, tough cafe situated close to Montreal's impressive Criminal Court buildings on Notre Dame Street.

The party settled itself far enough away from the four piece band to talk without having to shout when Gisele asked Jimmy quietly:

"What is a scandal monger?"

Both Sammy and Jimmy looked at her immediately. Neither said a word although they exchanged knowing glances.

Flustered she said, "Mister Courtney said that in this business one sometimes associated with the wrong types of people like . . . scandal mongers."

An oppressive silence fell on the table. Diane studied her fingernails intently while Sammy busied himself tearing the label from a beer bottle. Jimmy outlined a stain on the table cloth with a heavy lead pencil.

Sammy was first to speak. He looked straight at Jimmy and said, "Why don't you tell her? . . . you big jerk."

"I intend to." He answered grimly.

Turning to Gisele he held her hand tenderly. "Look Sugar Puss, it isn't easy to tell you this now that you are so happy at the Coq D'Or. You see," he paused to take a drink, "Courtney and I do not fall into the Damon and Pythias category. You probably don't understand so I'll just explain that we are not on friendly terms."

"But why Jimmy."

"It's a long story."

"A dirty one, too." Sammy broke in.

Jimmy ignored the interruption and continued. "Court-ney was mixed up in a rather notorious case some time ago. He wasn't convicted largely due to the ability of Quebec law-yers. I worked on the story and dug up some of the evidence used against him. He has hated me since."

Gisele looked puzzled. "But you are treated so well at the club. This I do not understand."

Sammy broke in again. "They wouldn't dare do other-wise."

Jimmy raised his hand for silence. "It's true Sugar Puss. I still cover the shows and Courtney and I nod politely at each other. But soon I'm going to dig up some data that will send him to Stoney Lonesome and this time it will take a battery of Philadelphia lawyers to keep him out."

She was startled by the hardness of his tone. His eyes narrowed to slits, and she wondered if there wasn't some-thing personal in the feud.

"Why do you write of such things, Jimmy?"

Jimmy touched a match to his cigarette before answering.

"I'd like to play in the same league as a friend of mine."

"Motion seconded." Sammy bounced his glass on the table.

Diane yawned prettily then turned to Sammy. "Look kid, there are plenty of sailors around here who look pretty attractive. Either you pay me some mind or I'm making me a date."

Sammy sighed. "Sorry, Princess. I yield before the mus-cled gentry."

For no apparent reason Jimmy laughed heartily. Calling a waiter he asked that the orchestra play "Claire de Lune."

The orchestra leader called an intermission and walked

over to the table. "It's a pleasure, Mister Holden." He bowed to the party and returned to the band stand.

He seated himself at the piano and glanced over its top at the gathering of prostitutes and petty thugs who frequented the tiny cafe. Then, closing his eyes tightly for a second, he shook his head and ran nimble fingers over the keys.

Gisele thought she detected a shudder as he started to play. The cafe quietened immediately as the haunting strains of the melody filled the room.

Streetwalkers tenderly held the hands of merchant seamen they fully intended to rob later in the evening. A grimy stevedore threatened with a glance a cab driver who placed his glass too noisily on the table.

Jimmy's eyes found Gisele's and held them. She knew he was re-living their precious moments at the Shuter Street apartment.

She couldn't tell when the song ended. There was a subdued murmur and then heavy applause reverberated through the room.

Jimmy leaned over to her and whispered. "We had better get a new record."

She didn't answer. His lips were close to hers and all else was oblivious. She kissed him boldly. No one gave them a second glance.

The piano player returned to the table and was introduced simply as "Ray." She noticed he called them all by their first names except Jimmy whom he respectfully addressed as "Mr. Holden."

Gisele glanced at his long tapered fingers and noticed they shook considerably.

Jimmy was eyeing him coldly. "When are you going to get smart, Ray?"

"You should not ask that question Mister Holden," he answered in a pained voice.

Gisele could not withhold her curiosity any longer. "What are you doing? A fine pianist like yourself, playing in a place of this type!"

"*Mam'selle*," Ray bowed. "If lectures could help I wouldn't be here."

"Ray drinks," said Jimmy flatly.

"Ray also takes dope." The piano player's voice was hard and bitter.

Jimmy shrugged his shoulders in a gesture that could mean anything or nothing. He made no further comment.

Ray stood up and bowed to Gisele. "Mister Holden is seldom wrong." He waited until a hard looking woman neared the table then bowed again and joined her. Together they walked to the rear of the club.

"There are too many 'strained silences' with this party." Sammy's voice was complaining.

"You're right again Honey. Let's get the hell out of here. This place gives me the willies." Diane was already on her feet ready to leave.

Jimmy handed the waiter a bill and they walked into the quietness of Notre Dame Street.

Sammy nodded toward Chateau de Ramezay. "Closed, Goddamn it. There goes our cultural pursuits for tonight."

"Let's go to The Breakers for some laughs." Diane was feeling better.

They piled into the first of a lengthy line of parked taxis and drove silently through Dead Man's Curve, past the towering financial buildings which line St. James Street then up Beaver Hill to Dorchester.

Gisele felt strangely at home as the cab sped along the now familiar street. Buildings that now were so familiar a few days before had been strange and practically forbidding.

They settled in a booth at The Breakers and Jimmy called for drinks. He stretched his long legs full length and leaned back sighing luxuriously.

Sammy excused himself and disappeared into the bar where he borrowed ten dollars from Big Jim Schultz.

Talk slowed down around the table. Jimmy untangled his legs from beneath the booth and walked over to the juke box. He thumbed a nickel into the slot and before he returned the strains of "Clair de Lune" filled the club.

Gisele watched him closely wondering whether or not Courtney's warning would change things for them. She regretted having told Jimmy anything about her conversation with the night club man but, she thought ruefully, it was too late to do anything about it now.

CHAPTER TWELVE

Dawn was lighting the sky when they said a belated 'good night' to Diane and Sammy then turned east on Dorchester. They had walked in silence to Stanley Street before Jimmy spoke.

"Sugar Puss. Have you seen much of Courtney since the night you met him?"

"Only twice Jimmy. Why do you ask?"

"I think he goes for you."

"That is quite impossible. I hardly know him and . . . well he has been most kind."

"His particular type of rodent is only kind when he wants something. I want you to keep away from him. You understand that, don't you?"

"I understand, Jimmy."

They reached the entrance to her rooming house and stood in awkward silence for a time. She looked into his troubled eyes and quelled a sudden desire to mother him.

"Shall we go upstairs, Jimmy?"

He didn't answer. Instead he held her firmly by the elbow and they mounted the stairs together. Reaching her door he held his hand out for the key and led her inside.

She slipped out of her clothes into a robe and walked to the shower room leaving him sitting on the bed struggling with a knotted shoe lace.

She fussed with the shades until she managed to arrange them in such a way that a shadow of the neon signs from Dorchester Street threw a beam across the bed. This accomplished she threw off her robe and lay expectantly on the covers.

She was debating in her mind whether or not to feign sleep when he returned. His jockey shorts were hanging from a hip pocket and his socks were clenched ball-like in his hand. He grinned at her. "That's a pretty classy shower, Sugar Puss."

She turned her head and smiled.

He folded his trousers carefully, reverse pleats even and the razor-like crease just so, over the chair. He probed into her closet until he found a hanger for his shirt then, draping his Countess Mara tie around the hook, he hung both on the lamp standard.

Impatiently she waited while he arranged his clothes. It seemed ages before he finally settled his wardrobe to his liking then slipped between sheets – his cool body close to her.

She ran her hand across his chest. "Why is it, Jimmy," she asked in a subdued tone, "that you have no hair on your chest although you are so . . . so . . . masculine?"

He kissed her before answering. "Why haven't you?"

She started to answer but laughed instead.

Both were serious. The light from Dorchester Street switched from red to green to red to green. They lay watching; their breathing audible now above the muffled sounds of the street.

"Gisele," his voice was huskily tender.

"Yes Jimmy?"

"Do . . . do you regret the other time?"

She looked up at his worried face. The lights were green now and she saw him as through a mist.

"No, Jimmy, I have no regrets."

"I didn't know that you were a . . ." He couldn't bring himself to say the word.

"I knew Jimmy. It is said that the first man is always the last man." He had to strain his ears to hear her, she spoke so softly. "It also means that you belong to me half the time – but I will belong to you all of the time. It is most confusing. I love you Jimmy."

He fell back on the pillow. "I love you too, Gisele. But had I known it would have been different."

Even in the dimly lit room she could see that his face showed signs of worry.

"Isn't it a bit late to think of it now, *Bébé*?" Her voice was soothing to his troubled mind.

He didn't answer. Instead he slid his arms under her shoulder and, clasping her tightly, drew her toward him.

In anticipation she ran her fingers through his hair. She found that she could draw him even closer to herself by pulling his face down to meet her own. She tried it and began breathing passionately.

The morning sun had replaced the neon lights when she awoke. She looked at Jimmy's sleeping form for a long moment before deciding that he was equally as handsome asleep or awake.

She rose and splashed cold water on her face then, donning slacks and a sweater, braved the heavy traffic on Dorchester Street to reach the restaurant directly opposite the rooming house.

Ignoring the obvious interest of the soda fountain clerk she bought cream cheese sandwiches and two large containers of coffee and carried them through the heavy traffic to the north side of the street.

She noted thankfully that Jimmy was still sleeping when she arrived. Placing the coffee and sandwiches on the chair she turned on the radio softly beside the sleeping form.

She ran her hand through his hair twice before he awakened. Leaning over she kissed him lightly and murmured, "Breakfast, Baby."

He looked about startled for a second then seeing her, grinned and said a cheery, "Good morning, Sugar Puss."

She handed him a container of coffee and a sandwich. "What time do you go to work?"

"Who knows in this unsettled world?" He grinned broadly.

There was a knock on the door and Gisele paled visibly. "Maybe it is the landlady," she whispered. "What will I do Jimmy?"

He laughed aloud. "So what. There are plenty of flea traps better than this one in Montreal. Go let her in."

Frightened, she opened the door slightly and peered out.

It was Sammy carrying four bottles of beer.

Almost weak with relief she looked at him in amusement as he fished an opener from his pocket and started uncorking the bottles.

"Why are you up before noon, Sammy?" she asked.

"Simple. Didn't go to bed." He reached for a sandwich and settled himself comfortably beside Jimmy.

She sat on the other side of the bed and listened intently to Sammy lecturing on the merits of beer for breakfast. He was, it seemed, a firm believer of such a practice.

The lecture was a lengthy one. After finishing his speech he announced that there was a shortage of beer and if they were a decent sort they would join him at the nearest bar and help overcome same shortage.

They dressed rapidly then walked west on Dorchester to Mountain where Sammy led them to a small basement bar which, Gisele learned, was a favorite hiding place during their many escapes from the attention of their city editor whom they referred to as "Beak Nose the Bloody."

It was a tiny intimate room done over in a marine decor. Life preservers hung around the walls and the windows were transformed into port holes. Fish nets served as curtains and a huge aquarium occupied the entire space behind the bar.

The three climbed on bar stools and ordered beer. They drank heartily for a time before Sammy announced sadly that he was off women for life.

"Maybe for two whole days, even," he said dismally.

Jimmy seemed uninterested. Wearily he asked. "Tell me all, Lover Boy."

Sammy looked at them sadly. "She weakened me. And my strength is as the strength of ten for my heart is pure. Am not going to see her again. Am writing an application to the first monastery I can think of." He returned to his beer, a picture of dejection.

"Too bad," Jimmy said. "Tried to make her and got the deep freeze treatment, huh?"

"No."

"Too expensive, huh? Likes to go to ritzy places which are too rich for your blood?"

"No."

"Oh."

"That's it. I find myself deeply in love. Not exactly a situation one can brush off then continue on one's merry way with full heart and firm tread. This is a calamity."

Jimmy gave him a crooked smile. "Why, pray tell, oh insane one?"

Even as the first rays of the morning's sun softly touched our recently cleaned Shuter Street abode I professed my love to her. And . . . she to me, also, too and in addition of."

"That bad?"

"That bad? Get him! Do you realize this means marriage? Patter of baby feet upon the unpaid-for linoleum. The little cottage in the Mount Royal covered with ivy and mortgages. Finance companies hounding you. Fresh linen every day. She'll probably even have me eating breakfast. That's for you. What's for me?"

He shook his head sadly and rose. Bowing to Gisele he muttered. "You see before you a broken man. I leave you with only memories . . . also the check."

He slowly climbed the stairs shaking his head sadly and uttering loud sobs into the handkerchief pressed against his face.

CHAPTER THIRTEEN

They ordered and drank another beer before Jimmy suggested walking her home. "I'll keep right on Dorchester and walk to the paper. Perhaps the fresh air will clear my head – I hope."

She nodded in agreement and they left the bar.

At the foot of the stairs leading to her rooming house he held her arm tightly.

"Gisele."

"Yes Jimmy."

"You're going to give your notice tonight, aren't you?"

"You mean you want me to quit the club?" She wanted to be certain she had not misunderstood his question.

"But Jimmy, what would I do if I left the chorus? I am making almost twice as much money as I would have had I remained a waitress. Also, the life is much more pleasant."

"You see, Sugar Puss, I'm doing pretty well. We won't starve."

"You mean you wish to marry me?"

"Well . . . not right away." He brushed a speck of lint from his lapel and avoided her eyes.

"Oh." Her voice came flat and listless.

"You see, Baby, I don't want you working for Courtney."

"Is that the only reason?"

"That's the only reason."

"He has treated me very well, Jimmy."

"You seem friendly toward him. Just how friendly did you get?"

It took her but a split second to grasp the implication then, in a sudden burst of fury, she slapped him across the face with as much strength as she could muster.

She watched his cheek take on a sudden reddish glow then, with a sob, she ran toward Stanley Street. A two-toned taxi was parked at the corner, its driver staring at them curiously. She jerked open the door and threw herself to the seat.

"Please hurry," she gasped.

The cab leaped forward immediately. Tires screamed in protest as it turned eastward. It careened through an amber light at the Peel Street intersection and sped toward the bridge at Metcalfe.

Halfway across the bridge the driver looked into the rear view mirror. "Where to, Miss?"

She glanced at him through tear-reddened eyes and answered, "Le Coq D'Or," without realizing why she said it.

The driver slackened his pace as they reached Beaver Hall Hill. Gisele worked frantically trying to remove traces of her crying spell.

She jumped from the cab even before it came to a complete stop and ran up the stairs of the club. Flinging open the doors she ran into the lobby to collide heavily with Gaston Courtney.

For a moment neither spoke. Courtney recovered first and gasped. "Obviously you are in a hurry Miss Lepine."

"I . . . I forgot something in the dressing room." She stammered.

"Well, Little One," his voice sounded paternal, "get it and perhaps you will join me in a drink, yes?"

Afraid to refuse she nodded and ran downstairs. Once inside the dressing room she put a damp towel over her face and lay quietly on the wardrobe trunk.

Courtney was sitting alone at the bar when she returned. She noticed that he sat with his twitching eye away from her. He didn't turn as she approached and she wondered if he was self-conscious of his affliction. At any rate, she thought, he had tact. He hadn't mentioned her tears.

They drank in silence then he led her across the street to the parking lot. He stopped before a chartreuse Cadillac convertible, inserted the key and held the door open for her.

"Have you had lunch?"

"No, *M'sieu* Courtney." She wondered why he always spoke to her in French.

"*Eh bien.* We shall go to my club and talk."

He guided the huge car into the west-bound traffic, drove as far as University then turned North. Soon they were crawling slowly along on the heavy east-bound traffic on Sherbrooke Street.

East of St. Lawrence he turned into a spacious driveway and parked before the entrance to what was once considered the most fashionable home in the city. Although the house was built before the turn of the century it still held to the air of elegance.

A tall hedge hid the driveway from the street and, Gisele noticed, maple trees added to the concealment of the upper story. Stained glass windows on either side of the imposing granite steps completed the scene surrounding the massive oak door.

The club was one of the few left in the city where a bank account was not considered as carte blanche by the membership secretary. This fact was impressed upon several of the many successful gamblers who had received polite notices by mail telling of the club's limited membership. Some, in fact, actually believed it.

Bartenders bowed as Courtney led Gisele to a tiny bar off the main hallway. He ordered a Martini for her then a Manhattan for himself. He sat twisting the glass by its delicate stem, his afflicted eye away from her. "I am very pleased with your performances at the club, Miss Lepine."

"Thank you. I like the work very much." She thought that he was not much younger than her own father. Very attractive too despite the nervous twitch of his eye. His grooming, she noted, was immaculate. But then . . . so was Jimmy's.

She drew her eyes from him in time to escape his noticing her interested gaze. With sudden interest she looked about the panelled walls and the intricate designs on the ceiling.

He smiled. "Am pleased that you are interested in this place. It was once the residence of one of Montreal's first families. We like to think that it is very exclusive."

"I think it is very beautiful."

After lunch they drove leisurely along Sherbrooke Street. Traffic had thinned out and the fashionable street took on that Fifth Avenue-ish look. At Guy Street he turned to her and casually asked. "Would you care to come up for a cocktail? I live only a short distance from here."

His invitation stunned her momentarily but before she could answer he smiled. "I do not have etchings, Little One. However I have a fine Picasso – although I do not know what it represents, plus a Dali, complete with liquid watch, which never fails to intrigue me."

She found herself laughing. Courtney, she thought, is interested. She had no qualms about going to his apartment. She felt she knew him far better than he realized. She smiled assent and he nodded his head pleasantly.

The car turned off the street, passed through a stone archway and came to a halt in a walled courtyard. Gisele's heart fluttered as she recognized the building. It was the towered apartment block of which she dreamed for five years.

She smiled to herself with self-satisfaction. Her plan was rapidly nearing completion. Although Jimmy's insult still seared her mind, the pain was alleviated by Courtney's obvious interest in her. And, she thought, as long as Jimmy believed she slept with Courtney – she may as well go through the motions. She wondered if she was beginning to hate Jimmy.

Courtney's apartment was on the 21st floor. It faced south and from its windows one could look over the city to the St. Lawrence. Gisele was fascinated. Her gaze swept from the Harbour Bridge to the Victoria. The sight of the ships plying between them thrilled her and she told Courtney so.

"The view is but one of the many reasons I chose this particular apartment." He bowed slightly and disappeared into an adjoining room.

Wandering through the apartment Gisele realized that this was what she had planned. Here was the luxury and, downstairs, a sleek automobile stood waiting. The Breakers and Jimmy Holden seemed very far away.

Courtney returned wearing a dinner jacket and they sat facing each other across a low coffee table. He clapped his hands twice and, almost immediately, a short squat Chinese appeared.

"A bottle of Cointreau, Kuo." Courtney addressed him in French.

As soon as the Oriental left the room Gisele turned wondrous eyes to Courtney and whispered. "He speaks French?"

"Fluently." Courtney seemed amused at her surprised look. "Also Spanish, German, Italian, Russian and, of course, English. Many years ago he decided wisely enough that he preferred being a well-paid servant to being a lawyer of uncertain income. He came to me straight from college and is invaluable."

Gisele's eyes remained serious. "Why do you always speak to me in French, *M'sieu* Courtney?" She expected him to say, 'please call me Gaston' – but he didn't.

Instead he replied, "Because I hope to extract the patois from your speech. It is time you learned to speak your native tongue correctly."

She lowered her eyes in embarrassment and wondered whether it would spoil anything if she were to get angry with him. Too close to the things she dreamed about, she decided.

Her teeth chewed her lower lip and she found herself getting angry – not with Courtney but with herself. How could she have overlooked such a thing. Her manners and her almost flawless English had been acquired only through years of concentration. And yet she had forgotten that her French was shot through with expressions peculiar to the Parisian inasmuch as they were pure 'Quebecois.'

Kuo mercifully broke the tension by re-appearing bearing a tray with a cut glass decanter and two glasses. He set them noiselessly on the coffee table and once more disappeared.

They sipped their drinks slowly for some time before he reached over and patted her hand affectionately.

"Perhaps, my dear, I should have told you that with more tact. But you must understand that it is all part of your grooming."

"My grooming? For what am I being groomed?"

Courtney rubbed his hand over his affected eye. "For your role as Madame Courtney. You see, Little One, I hope to make you my wife as soon as it is possible. That is, of course, if you are willing. If you accept my proposal."

"But you have not proposed to me as yet."

"My dear I have just finished proposing to you. Maybe my offer was not the one you would expect but I am not a romantic young fool. It was Mayor Houde, I believe, who first uttered the classic: "Too many persons get married for better or for worse – but not enough for good."

He smiled and leaned over to hold her hand in a firm grip. "Our marriage will last, Gisele. We are both French and neither of us are overly romantic. Our life together will be pleasant."

He reached inside his jacket and withdrew a large velvet case which he handed to her. "An engagement present, my darling."

With trembling fingers she released the catch and the box flew open to reveal a small platinum wrist watch. The band was thick and exquisitely worked with delicate scrolls. Diamond chips replaced numerals on the face.

Clapping his hands once more to summon Kuo he turned to her and said, "You will meet me after the final performance at the club. Kuo will drive you there now."

CHAPTER FOURTEEN

As Kuo guided the huge car through the streets Gisele pondered over her attachment to Courtney. She was not so naïve as to think the middle aged man was madly in love with her. There was no passion; no emotional upheaval. Nothing but a pleasant, comfortable arrangement in which she would obtain a social position, wealth and security whilst he would gain a wife – young, beautiful and, no doubt, polished under his tutelage.

His offer of marriage was flattering. She had been certain that there would be a preliminary advance. Sitting amid the luxury of the Cadillac she pondered. "I wonder what he will do. And I wonder what I will do – if he will do what I am wondering he will do."

She looked at the watch for the twelfth time. The girls would soon be arriving at the club and, for some reason, she didn't want them to be around when she drove up in Courtney's car.

She studied Kuo's well-tailored back. Suddenly she wanted him to let her off around the corner from the club. She decided against this plan as she realized the faithful Kuo, frantically loyal to his employer, would, no doubt, report to him all irregularities.

The Oriental eased the car to the curb exactly opposite the club entrance. Gisele saw several of the girls and their escorts loitering before the brilliantly lighted marque. Too late to turn back now, she thought. Kuo had already climbed from the car and was reaching for the door handle and ready to help her alight.

She spotted Sammy and Diane among the crowd and guessed that the entire chorus had been out on a mass date before coming to the club for the first show. Sammy was gesticulating wildly before a stern-faced Diane. Trixie's boyfriend was shouting odds on the forthcoming battle. "Eight to five on the little lady," he screamed. Everyone seemed reasonably drunk.

Gisele took a deep breath stepping from the car. Her arrival was greeted by a sudden silence and all eyes turned toward her.

She paused, embarrassed, before the group. Even Sammy was strangely quiet. Gisele wondered if she should continue into the club and make some sort of an explanation later. This, however, would only make the situation appear worse. Her voice almost reached the breaking point as she stuttered a few 'hellos.'

It was Trixie who first spoke. "Well," she said, her voice heavy with sarcasm, "not bad for a country bumpkin. The boss's car yet. Get this kid!"

The feeling of hostility within the group was being felt when Sammy broke the spell. "Cinderella, Baby, you're not due until midnight – and that Caddy is one helluva substitute for a punkin' coach."

The men laughed – but not as heartily as Gisele had hoped. The girls' silence was embarrassing. It made her feel like a prostitute caught in the act.

She noted with relief that Jimmy was not among the crowd. She was tempted to ask Sammy of his whereabouts but pride overcame her curiosity.

A brief period of conversation followed as the girls automatically promised to meet the boys as soon as the first show was over.

Gisele sat before her space at the dressing room table. Her fingers ran nimbly over her costume and her hair, adjusting a strap here and there and twisting a curl into place beneath the picture hat which was worn for the first number.

The feeling of coolness could not escape her. The usual chatter was missing from the room as the girls made up and dressed. The silence pounded against her brain. She knew it was caused by her presence – her presence alone. The girls were resentful of her. She felt miserable.

As each avoided her gaze she realized that she was a marked woman. She knew that they guessed she was sleeping with Courtney. That figured, she thought, that it was a matter of economics; that Courtney had money – that Jimmy hadn't. It was as simple as that . . . so they thought.

She longed to tell them that Courtney was merely the target of a lengthy campaign. That his social position and his wealth was something on which she planned through five frustrating years.

She realized they liked Jimmy. His obsession for fine clothes. His razor-edge wit. His loyalty to his friends. He was well-loved among show people and respected by those who came in contact with him.

The fanfare thundered from upstairs and the girls hastened to make final adjustments to themselves and their costumes. Gisele drew a deep breath and walked quickly through the dressing room.

Her cheeks burned with indignation as she lined up behind the curtain. She thought of what was at stake – the apartment, the security, the social position.

The girls were staring straight ahead. Gisele felt a bit panicky. She tried to relax. "You're too close to quit now," she thought.

She felt someone nudge her and turned to stare into Diane's serious face. Gisele turned her head away. Diane's voice came to her over the din of the orchestra. "What are you building, Kid?"

Gisele didn't answer. The curtains parted and the chorus moved out onto the floor. Further conversation was impossible as the routine continued to a fast and furious finale. Impatiently the chorus waited until the curtain had closed shutting them off from the audience then, as one, they dashed madly down the stairs to the dressing room.

The numbers seemed endless to Gisele. She danced automatically and dreaded the intervals in the dressing room.

At last the final show came and went and the chorus dressed hastily in street clothes. Gisele was slipping into her shoes when Diane broke the icy silence of the room. "Want to speak to you Frenchy." Her voice was low and strained.

Gisele nodded and silently followed her up the stairs. She was halfway when she realized she hadn't bid her customary 'good night' to the others. Too late to turn back now. That would be too obvious a gesture.

Instead she followed Diane to a ringside table at which Sammy sat alone. Not too alone, however. He held a glass of rye in each hand and was addressing them in serious tones.

As they joined him he placed the glasses on the table, rose, bowed and beckoned a waiter all in one movement.

Gisele looked about the club. Jimmy, she noticed, was not present at his usual table. She felt a tinge of disappointment mingled with a deep feeling of relief.

Sammy sensed the object of her gaze. "He's busy slaving over a hot typewriter, Sugar Puss."

Gisele decided Sammy was a very poor liar, but she didn't comment on the explanation.

Diane suddenly grasped her by the wrist. "Look, Gisele, it's none of my business and you don't have to answer if you don't want to but . . . what's with this Courtney guy and you. What's with this chauffer-driven Cadillac? What's with this little Tiffany trinket?" she fingered the watch on Gisele's wrist.

"Oh . . . that?" Gisele detected the false ring to her own voice with discomfort. "Mr. Courtney gave it to me. He's very kind." She tried to smile but the effort was too great.

Diane shook her head sadly. "If Jimmy sees that he'll have pups right in the editorial department."

"Perhaps it's none of Jimmy's business." Gisele's voice was low and grim.

There was a lengthy silence finally broken by Diane's quiet, "Oh."

Sammy coughed nervously then, excusing himself, left the table to join a group of newspaper boys who clung to the bar.

Diane watched his retreating figure and waited until he joined in deep conversation with them before turning back to Gisele.

"I hope you know what you're doing, Baby."

"I think I do, Diane."

"People are going to talk, Frenchy. People always do you know. It will be tough being on the receiving end."

"What people say – or think – does not concern me, Diane. I know what I want and, I assure you, I know where I am going. So please do not be alarmed."

Diane's voice lacked enthusiasm. "Well I guess, as long as you know what you are doing . . ."

Suddenly Gisele grew angry. "Why should everyone be so interested in my personal affairs? Do I comment on the behaviour of the other girls? Am I so different that I cannot choose my own friends?" Her anger mounted as did the color in her face. She broke into French in her excitement.

Embarrassed, she apologized to Diane and explained that her French phrases were not spoken in anger but in excitement.

Diane leaned back in her chair. Her eyes swept over Gisele's face. "Shush," she said in a tired voice. "You should realize by now how things stand between Jimmy and Courtney. The boss would gladly have Jimmy taken care of – if he dared. Courtney is afraid of him and everybody in town knows it. That is, everybody but you, apparently."

Sammy returned to the table all too soon. His eyes were shining partly with pleasure and partly from the effects of hastily gulped double ryes.

"Hows about joining Father Hoffman at the Chicken Palace for spare ribs? Just borrowed a sawbuck from the boys and I do hereby solemnly promise to pay the bill myself . . . personally and promptly."

Diane smacked her lips in a decidedly unladylike manner. "Spare ribs? That's for me. What about you Gisele?"

Gisele shook her head. "I'm so sorry. I have a date."

Diane's pretty face became suddenly bitter. "Courtney?"

Gisele nodded and left the table.

Sammy quickly blocked her way. He looked deep into her troubled eyes and smiled, "I don't know what it's all about Sugar Puss – but play it your way. If you get your fingers burnt come cry on Uncle Sammy's shoulder." He held out the lapel of his coat. "Look! A Maxie the Burglar special – guaranteed not to shrink."

Urged by a sudden impulse she kissed him lightly on the cheek just as Kuo approached, hat in hand, to tell her the car was waiting.

She felt a dozen pair of hostile eyes boring into her back as she threaded her way through the milling crowd past the bar where the entire chorus was gathered.

She slid quickly into the rear seat and prayed that Kuo would drive away from the club as fast as possible. Then her mood changed. She fought back an impulse to jump from the car and run back to Sammy and Diane. Suddenly she wanted to be a part of the chorus and share spare ribs at the Chicken Palace. Perhaps Sammy would call Jimmy and everything would be as it was before.

Realizing that this was too much to hope for she leaned back heavily against the cushions. Jimmy, she thought, would now regard her in a different light. She had little doubt but that he considered her Courtney's mistress. Nothing could ever be as it was before their first – and last – fight. She wanted to cry.

Kuo turned slightly in his seat. "Mister Courtney instructed me to pick up your things, Miss Lepine." He spoke in flawless French.

Dumbfounded she led the chauffeur up the stairs and automatically pointed out the janitor's apartment to him. She heard his voice as she slowly mounted the stairs. He said, "Miss Lepine is leaving. Please . . . the bill."

"Play it your way," Sammy had told her but she wondered if Sammy had ever found himself involved in a situation as intricate as this. She guessed not.

Events were piling up too fast for her to cope with. She couldn't think clearly. She closed her eyes tightly and shook her head to free some of the turmoil that raged within. "This is what you wanted. This is what you're getting. Nothing comes easily." Her thoughts were spoken aloud.

She leaned against the wall of the room and watched Kuo pack her things rapidly and expertly. She felt she would feel homesick once she left this room. It had been her first home in the city and it was but a few hours ago that she and Jimmy . . .

Before Kuo drove the shiny car from the curb Gisele looked longingly at the grimy entrance to what was her lodgings. She wanted desperately to go back but knew that that was an impossibility. She neither knew nor cared where Kuo was taking her. This was the beginning, she told herself. This was the preview to the real thing.

The car drew up before the club where Courtney had taken her to lunch that afternoon. A uniformed doorman escorted her to the tiny bar where Courtney was seated. Two men were with him and the three were engaged in earnest conversation.

Courtney rose as she entered. He crossed the bar to take her hand and lead her to the table. "You look lovely, my dear," his voice was rich with pride.

Still holding her hand he introduced her to the two men at the table, "*Voilà*," he smiled triumphantly, "the reason I remained a bachelor these many years."

Remembering his remark concerning her French, Gisele spoke slowly and distinctly during the few times she joined the small talk around the table. The men, she learned, were Courtney's lawyers and their talk revolved mainly around libel laws, inheritance regulations and defamation of character suits.

Conversation soon bogged down and Gisele felt that the men were not talking openly because of her presence. It seemed ages before Courtney rose and, bidding good night to the two men, took Gisele by the arm and led her from the club.

Kuo was waiting in the car when they left through the side entrance. Courtney helped her into the seat and placed her arm through his own. "Home, Kuo," he said happily. For the first time Gisele was frightened . . . and showed it.

He looked at her sharply. "There is still nothing to fear, Little One."

Arm in arm they walked down the corridor in the direction of his apartment. Gisele was close to shaking in fear of the immediate future. Instead of stopping at his own apartment, however, Courtney passed on to the one adjoining it. He inserted the key and stood back holding the door open for her.

"This is yours."

The apartment was a replica of his except that it was decidedly feminine. Lavishly furnished, it retained, somehow, an atmosphere of good taste. Gisele wandered through the three rooms. Pausing in the luxurious bedroom she told herself, "The plan is almost completed."

She now regretted the days spent with Jimmy. Few though they had been they somehow took the edge off the happiness she knew she should feel at this moment. Perhaps, she thought, she had given herself too soon. Perhaps, had she waited, she could bring herself to hold a similar feeling for this middle-aged man who wanted her as his wife.

"Fool," she muttered to herself and turned to embrace the waiting Courtney with a tenderness that surprised them both.

He kissed her with restraint then broke free. Handing her a set of keys he pointed to these for the apartment and the smaller ones which, he explained, were for the car.

"The car, of course, will be downstairs at all times. I have another."

Looking at his watch he kissed her lightly once more. "I'll see you tomorrow my dear," he sounded impatient as he quickly strode from the apartment.

Gisele unpacked then sat looking at the skyline.

CHAPTER FIFTEEN

She awoke just in time to see a tall dark girl dressed in the uniform of a maid pull back the drapes flooding the room with sunlight.

The maid turned and looked at her steadily, "I'm Therese."

Gisele nodded but said nothing.

Therese patted the pillows in place behind Gisele's back then speaking in French, said, "I will bring your breakfast immediately, *Mam'selle*." She paused at the door and, still speaking in French, added, "Madame Lapointe will be here within the hour."

"Madame Lapointe?"

"The modiste, *Mam'selle*."

Again Gisele nodded but said nothing. Propped up on the pillows and surrounded by more luxury than she thought possible and with the prospect of breakfast in bed she considered the mere visit of a modiste as very anti-climactic indeed.

Therese returned carrying a tray which she set on a table over Gisele's lap. Gisele started comparing this breakfast with the one Jimmy had brought to her in paper bags at the Dorchester Street room.

She was sad for a moment then brushed the memory from her mind. She made a resolution knowing she would not keep it, that she would stop thinking of Jimmy. She was still thinking of him, however, when Madame Lapointe flounced in followed by an entourage of assistants.

The modiste, a huge woman, looked very much as if a few of her own fabulous creations could be used to advantage on her own ample frame.

She surveyed Gisele critically from every angle and explained, through a mouth filled with pins, that Monsieur

Courtney had ordered several gowns. He had guessed at the size and "if *Mam'selle* would cease wriggling in such a manner, she would have them altered and delivered that very afternoon."

After two hours of modelling clothes that would be her own, Gisele grew happily tired. Courtney's impeccable taste, she noted, included women's fashions.

Madame Lapointe had given the nearest possible example of a human being sparked with atomic power. At one point she had seized Gisele's shoes and snorted in disgust. Striding to the telephone she had called a Sherbrooke Street shoe store. An ultra exclusive one. Gisele listened with amusement as the amazonic creature explained the color combination she required. She ranted and raved and extracted a promise of immediate delivery. Madame Lapointe was explosive and her temper is described in French as being "*formidable.*"

Within a half hour twenty pairs of shoes were scattered about the already cluttered floor. The Madame berated the delivery boy – who shrunk back in terror – and told him to return four pairs as they "were not fit for a cow to wear in an obscure meadow at midnight."

The room seemed strangely empty when Madame Lapointe left. Gisele examined the sixteen remaining pairs of shoes and the countless dresses which, through dint of Madame Lapointe's nimble fingers coupled with Courtney's amazing guesswork, were considered suitable for Gisele to wear in public.

She tried on each of the gowns in turn trying to remember the modiste's instructions as to which pair of shoes went with each dress.

She soon tired of this and walked leisurely into the kitchen. Therese was busily washing dishes.

"Is Monsieur Courtney at home?" she asked the maid.

"Monsieur Courtney went out of town last night, *Mam'-selle*. He left a parcel and a note for you on the hall stand, *Mam'selle*."

Pleased with his thoughtfulness Gisele took the parcel from the stand and sat on the side of her bed in eager anticipation. The package contained a heavy set of matched compact, neckpiece and bracelet. The note read: "Wear them tonight, Little One." It was signed 'Gaston.'

Gisele fondled the pieces. The bracelet was made up of three-quarter inch gold blocks which circled her wrist twice. The neckpiece was identical except that it was longer and could be draped in two strands around her neck. The compact was thick and heavy and delicately engraved to her.

She put the bracelet and neckpiece on and looked with admiration in the mirror. This was indeed a happy day, she decided. Too happy to stay at home and gloat over her possessions. "I will go for a drive. I will get that feeling of luxury behind the wheel of the car." She was talking aloud not caring if Therese heard her or not.

Wrapping a bandanna show-girl-like around her hair she found the keys Courtney had given her and left the apartment.

Driving the convertible was a new thrill. She handled it like a veteran and made a mental note to thank Jackie, the resort comedian, who first taught her to drive. She slid the car into the west-bound traffic on Sherbrooke Street and headed for Decarie Boulevard. She now called it the "Sunset Strip," an expression she had picked up from the crowd at the club.

She drove a few miles north then turned into a combination hot dog stand, curb service restaurant and swimming pool. She ordered a hamburger and coke and sat idly watching the swimmers disport themselves in the crystal clear water of the spacious tank.

A strong sun cast shimmering reflections on the water so Gisele left the car to buy a pair of sunglasses. "Now I'm really a show girl," she told herself.

She drove slowly to the corner of Sherbrooke and Guy streets wondering if she should call on Diane. She was feeling too happy to allow any hostility to spoil the picture. Perhaps she could explain to both Diane and Trixie that she had planned this venture five years ago. It would be easier to tell them. They lived together and would no doubt understand her position. She wished she lived with one of the girls. Were this so, everything would be pleasant. She would tell her roommate her problems and her roommate in turn would tell the rest of the chorus. In this way there would be understanding instead of this stupid hostility.

She made a left hand turn at the Guy and Sherbrooke corner and made a mental note to explain the inevitable ticket to Courtney. Parking outside a Mansfield Street apartment block she ran quickly up the stairs and knocked on the door of No. 312. Trixie's deep-throated voice wafted from inside. "Just a minute."

The door was pulled open and Trixie met her with surprise. "Well, Cinderella herself. C'mon in and we'll open up a can of worms."

Diane came out of the shower room, a bath towel wrapped turban-like around her head. "Surprise, surprise," she chirped. "And what brings you to our humble abode at this time of day, Sugar Puss?"

Gisele felt uncomfortable and a bit sorry that she had come. "About last night," she stammered timidly, "It isn't the way you think . . ."

"Is there another way?" Trixie's voice was heavy with sarcasm. She sat cross-legged on the divan manicuring her nails with a foot-long file.

Gisele's spirits dropped and she ran to the door.

"Just a minute, Kid," Diane called in a friendly tone.

Gisele held her hand on the door knob but turned as Diane spoke. "You know, Sugar Puss, there's plenty of jealousy in every chorus and these old bags are plenty hot because you hooked the biggest fish available in the local pond. Courtney never gave any of his chorines a tumble – that is, until you came along."

Trixie held her hand at arm's length and studiously regarded her finger nails. "Yeah, that's part of it," she said, "but there's always the case of one Jimmy Holden."

"Jimmy is well liked," Diane put in solemnly, "and the fact that you dropped him for bigger game is a bit too much. We just didn't think you were the type, that's all."

Gisele ignored the obvious invitation to explain. Instead she asked flatly. "How is Jimmy?"

"No one has seem him around lately. Sammy says he is working on a special assignment. He says Beak Nose the Bloody – what a helluva name to call a guy – gave Jimmy a free hand on a story."

There was a sound of footsteps in the hall. Sammy burst into the room flushed and excited. He gasped, "Have you seen . . ."

He stopped short when he saw Gisele. Grabbing her roughly by the arm he demanded, "Is that Courtney's car downstairs?"

She knew by his worried face that he was not playing one of his usual jokes. She nodded "yes."

"Gimme the keys."

She handed them over without protest.

Sammy thrust a copy of the first edition *Chronicle* at her and ran from the room.

Three pairs of eyes watched him go. Trixie sat in silence, her nail file held upright; Diane, stupefied, was holding the bath towel on her head; Gisele looked dazedly at the newspaper Sammy had forced into her hand.

Finally Trixie broke the silence with, "What in hell do you suppose got into him?"

Diane shook her head dumbly. Gisele smoothed out the newspaper. The inky black headlines screamed out at her:

VICE LORD SUSPECT
SOUGHT IN SLAYING
Seek Gaston Courtney
In Policeman's Death
– by Jimmy Holden –

Gaston Courtney, wealthy night club operator and suspected kingpin of local white slave traffic, was still at large at an early hour this afternoon. He is wanted for questioning in the death of Constable Andre Dupuis, 32, of Rosemont, and in the wounding of Constable Pierre Daoust, 29, of St. Henri, following a furious gun battle shortly before noon today. The battle took place on Dorchester Street West before the horrified gazes of hundreds of passers by.

Orders to pick up Courtney for questioning in regards to vice operations in the city were relayed to all police officers at 11:35 a.m. this morning. New evidence of Courtney's connections with the underworld was presented to police headquarters shortly before the dragnet was ordered.

According to eye witnesses the two police victims approached a black sedan parked on Dorchester Street near the intersection of Guy at about noon. As the officers neared the vehicle a man, answering to Courtney's description, leaned forward from the rear window and pumped two shots at the policemen. Constable Dupuis died almost immediately but Constable Daoust, although severely wounded, returned the fire.

A passing police cruiser came on the scene almost immediately but lost the sedan after a wild chase which ended on Bishop Street near Sherbrooke. The sedan was driven by a man believed to be of Chinese origin.

Gisele pressed her hands to her cheeks and screamed. The paper fell to the floor where both Trixie and Diane pounced upon it and, in wide-eyed wonder, read the front page.

A fear-filled fog spread across the room. They looked at each other in terror. Gisele fought off an attack of hysterics.

Trixie's voice came through the spell. She said, "So? So let's have a drink."

The cheap rye burned Gisele's throat and brought tears to her eyes. "What shall I do?" She repeated the question over and over.

Presently Sammy returned. Without a word he walked over to Trixie and took the bottle from her hand and poured himself a drink. He then turned to Gisele and placed a hand on her shoulder.

"You realize, Sugar Puss, that the coppers are looking for you too."

"But . . . but why do they want me, Sammy?"

"You were spotted driving Courtney's car out on the Strip earlier today. That's why I took the car and parked it in the garage under our place on Shuter Street."

"But I haven't done anything wrong, Sammy." Her voice was pleading.

"They want you for questioning. You must realize that they know you occupy the apartment next to his. In fact they have already searched your place."

He suddenly jumped to his feet. "My God!" he shouted. "Quick, Diane, get some of your clothes on Gisele. She's got to get out of here right now! Trixie! You phone Mike at The

Breakers and tell him to bring his cab to the back entrance."

The girls hastened to do what he ordered. No one thought of disobeying him.

Gisele hurriedly climbed into a dress of Diane's. Trixie contacted Mike. Sammy explained that all their apartments would be searched for Gisele.

Soon Mike's Slavic features peered through the door. His eyes expressed appreciation of Trixie's shape and he smiled shyly as she handed him a drink.

Once inside his cab Mike gave his mind over to driving as fast as possible. In the back seat Sammy handed Gisele a newspaper. "Make like you're near-sighted, Baby. Up close to the face." He gave Mike instructions on how to get to the garage under the Shuter Street apartment.

Once inside the apartment Gisele threw herself on the bed and wept silently. Sammy ignored her and went into the kitchen in search of a drink.

CHAPTER SIXTEEN

The telephone jangled from beneath the bed.

Sammy dashed from the kitchen, spilling his drink as he did so, quickly grabbed the receiver and shouted, "Hello."

He listened without interruption for some time. Finally he said, "She's here. I'll tell her."

He replaced the receiver on the hook and turned to Gisele. "That was Jimmy. He says for you to wait until he gets here. He says not to move from here. He's at police headquarters."

As if in a trance she nodded at Sammy and moved only when he brought her a drink. They sat side by side in silence awaiting Jimmy's arrival.

When Jimmy finally arrived Gisele was shocked at his appearance. The three top buttons of his shirt were loose and the strings of his bow tie rested on his chest. His suit was rumpled and she guessed his beard was in its third day. His eyes were red-rimmed and tired and she held back the urge to gather him in her arms.

He greeted her coolly as he stripped off his shirt. "Hello Sugar Puss." She wondered if she heard a tinge of sarcasm in his tone.

He disappeared into the kitchen and reappeared shortly carrying a bottle of beer and a glass. Pouring himself a drink he looked at her from over the rim of the glass.

"Baby," he said grimly, "you and I are going to sit here and have a little *tete-a-tete*."

Sammy wriggled into his jacket. "Why speak of work when there's love to be done. Othello . . . Ol' Fellow," he left the apartment still clutching his glass.

As soon as the door closed behind Sammy, Jimmy grasped Gisele's arm tightly. "When did you last see Courtney?" His voice was as stern as she had ever heard it.

"Last night after the show."

"Where did you go with him?"

"I met him at his club and then we went to the ... apartment."

"Whose apartment?"

She lowered her eyes to escape his searching gaze. "The apartment he gave me."

"What else did he give you?" His voice was accusing.

She didn't answer.

"Did you sleep with him last night?"

She half turned and slapped him. Hard.

"Does that answer your question?"

She was halfway down the narrow hallway before he caught her. His hand buried itself in her arm and she fought as he half pushed, half dragged her back to the bed. He pushed her violently and she fell cursing him in French.

"That's two I owe you. Let us have no more dramatics," he said quietly.

She lay panting. Her hatred for him frightened her. Her eyes narrowed to slits as she watched him pacing the floor.

Finally he brought her a glass and poured beer in it. Holding her hand he asked gently. "Why did you do it?"

"Why did I do what?" she spat the words out between clenched teeth.

"Go out with Courtney."

"If I told you it was part of a plan you would not believe me. You once told me you loved me. I believed you. Now I know that you lied. You are in love with a newspaper. That, I do not wish to compete with."

"You didn't answer my question."

"You are wondering if I was Courtney's mistress, are you not? Why do you ask so many questions when there is but one answer you are seeking? I did not sleep with Courtney. I did not sleep with anyone . . . except you."

He pulled her to him roughly. "You're in a jam, Sugar Puss."

"Why should I be in this thing which you call a 'jam'? I have shot no policemen. I know nothing of this white slave business. Why, then, am I in this jam?"

"That, Baby, is only part of the story. Courtney is wanted on a dope charge. The police are withholding information for the time being. They had hoped Courtney would face the white slavery charge knowing he could beat it easily. However, when the shooting started he, no doubt, believed they had proof of his narcotic dealings. Otherwise he would have reported to police headquarters and . . . one damn fine cop would still be alive."

"You haven't told me why the police want to speak to me."

He encircled her wrist drawing her toward him. "Gisele, you're tabbed as Courtney's mistress. It is known that he was carrying a large cache of dope with him. A search of his apartment and . . . yours . . . revealed nothing."

"It is very unlikely he would carry the stuff with him. Therefore someone close to him must have it. You, Sugar Puss, are the logical suspect. Someone took the stuff from his apartment. Who else could do it as easily as you?"

Suddenly the seriousness of her plight dawned upon her. She clutched him violently and buried her face on his shoulders in an effort to keep from screaming. He pushed her back and slapped her sharply.

"For Christ's sake don't get hysterical on me."

She started to sob again. Desperately she tried to figure a means of escape from the net she felt was drawing closer and closer about her.

Home. That was where she wanted to be. Home. St. Christophe and her attic bedroom. No one would think of looking for her there. Even if they did, she thought, the villagers would never let them take her. She must go, she reasoned. She must go – now.

Jimmy shook her. "You're safe here, Sugar Puss. This is one place they'll never think of looking for you. Now, tell me everything that happened last night."

Suddenly she was calm again. "Nothing happened, Jimmy. He . . . Monsieur Courtney . . . showed me my new apartment and then he left. I woke up this morning and a modiste fitted me with some new gowns. I asked the maid where he was and she told me he had gone out of town. He left me a note and some presents . . ."

Jimmy jumped to his feet. "Where are the presents?" He almost screamed at her.

"Why . . . here." She fingered the neckpiece and bracelet.

He snatched the neckpiece from her throat and examined it closely. He tried biting one of the gold cubes without success. Finally he placed it on the table and brought a can opener and a can of soup from the kitchen.

She watched him with fascination as he placed the pointed prong of the opener on the cube and hammered it with the can of soup. On the third blow the prong disappeared into the cube.

Jimmy then picked up the neckpiece carefully and placed it over an ashtray. Gently tapping the side away from the puncture he grinned widely as a snowy-white powder flowed into the ashtray.

He was still grinning as he repeated the process with her bracelet and compact. Each contained powder.

Finally he sat down heavily beside her, his eyes transfixed on the jewelry. "Well I'll be a son of a . . ."

Gisele's eyes widened in astonishment. She looked at him for an explanation.

"See what I mean, Sugar Puss?" He fingered the bracelet.

"That is . . . what the police are looking for?"

He nodded.

"What is going to happen now, Jimmy?"

"I wish I knew. There is a fortune of the stuff here and, chances are, Courtney is looking for you just as eagerly as are the police. Believe me, it would be far better if the police find you first."

He fingered the bracelet thoughtfully. "I think I can work a deal, maybe." He rose and put on his jacket. "Stay here until I get back."

"No. Don't leave me." She screamed her protest.

He clapped a hand over her mouth. "What do you mean? No. Stay here."

She struggled free. "Jimmy, I am going home."

"Home?" He raised an eyebrow as he asked the question.

"St. Christophe."

"Are you out of your stinkin' mind?"

"I am going. That is all. I am going."

She didn't see the blow coming until it was too late to avoid. It caught her neatly on the left jaw and she collapsed without a sound. He picked her up from the floor and placed her on the bed. Kissing her lightly on the lips he ran from the apartment.

Gisele awoke not knowing how long she had been unconscious.

With an effort she reached the bathroom and splashed cold water on her face and massaged her aching jaw.

The coldness revived her somewhat and she recalled suddenly that Jimmy had hit her. Panic rose within her as she realized she was alone in the apartment. A trap, she thought, terror-stricken.

After a moment's hesitation she opened the door cautiously and peered out. The corridor was empty. She ran frantically down the three flights of stairs that led to the basement garage.

Inky blackness smote her as she pushed open the door. Pressing her body against the wall she waited impatiently for her eyes to grow accustomed to the darkness. Soon she made out the dark shadow of the convertible. It was parked against the far wall.

Praying that Sammy had left the keys in the ignition she raced across the garage and slid in behind the wheel. Just as her groping fingers reached the dashboard she saw Kuo.

She opened her mouth to scream just as a yellow hand pressed across her face, cutting off her breath. From the corner of her eye she saw a snub nosed revolver being raised . . . then lowered and flashes of lightening seared her brain as she slipped into unconsciousness over the steering wheel.

CHAPTER SEVENTEEN

Jimmy hailed a cab at the corner of Shuter and Sherbrooke then fidgeted while the driver cursed and fought his way through the dense traffic to police headquarters.

He left the cab at the front entrance but ran around to the side of the building where a narrow entrance opened off to the street. He raced up the stairs to the third floor and barged into the door marked Homicide Squad.

Chief Inspector Lawson was studying a map of the city when Jimmy burst in. The chief turned and smiled then spoke to the three detectives who were intently regarding the map.

"Courtney will no doubt try to leave the island by the southern route." The chief's voice droned on. "His one chance of escape is to get across the border near Rouses Point then make a dash for El Paso, Texas, then across to Juarez, Mexico. That's his one chance and the only logical one. Therefore we must be prepared for a surprise.

"Escape via the U.S. is too obvious. Only a fool would try it . . . and Courtney is no fool."

Jimmy waited impatiently as the Inspector detailed the detectives to various points. When at last they were alone he threw Gisele's presents on the desk. "There's the loot, Bill."

The Chief picked up the jewelry and inspected it piece by piece. He noticed the pierced cubes and tapped them lightly. A thin stream of powder trickled out onto his desk blotter. His face remained inscrutable.

"Where did you find it, Jimmy?" He spoke as if he wouldn't be surprised if his question was ignored.

"It's a long story, Bill."

"No doubt." He walked leisurely to the window.

"You know Jimmy, when newspapermen start playing detectives there is always a backfire. Usually bad."

"We did all right the last time, Bill."

"This is no cheap gambling feud, Jimmy – you should know that."

The telephone interrupted Jimmy's answer. Lawson picked up the receiver. "Lawson here. Where? Going north on St. Denis near Cremazie? Right." He slammed down the phone and barked crisp instructions into his desk microphone.

Turning to Jimmy, who sat tensely on the edge of a chair, he said calmly. "The boys have spotted Courtney's car. They think Courtney was driving but are not quite sure, it was travelling too fast. They saw a girl in the front seat."

"A girl?" Jimmy grabbed the phone and frantically dialed the apartment. The phone buzzed monotonously. No answer. He threw the receiver back on its hook and stared at the Chief.

"She's innocent, Bill. I swear it."

"Relax, Jimmy. Let's try to keep her alive long enough to prove it." He snapped on the microphone and detailed extra men to the search, then turned back to the map.

Without looking at Jimmy he asked. "Where did you first dig up the information on Courtney, Kid?"

"From a hopped-up piano player I know. He works in one of those dives on Notre Dame Street. It took a bit of talking and a lot of time spent around there and up at Clarke and St. Catherine before I finally narrowed down the suspects to Courtney."

"You, of course, know the girl involved."

"She's fresh from a farm, Bill. She doesn't know what goes on." Jimmy started to pace the floor. He felt unhappy and frustrated in the knowledge that he could do nothing but wait.

The telephone rang again. Chief Lawson listened intently. "South on Papineau near Ontario?" He snapped on the desk mike and ordered the northern end of the Harbour Bridge patrolled.

"We'll get him Jimmy . . . alive, I hope."

Jimmy nodded dismally. "Who in hell cares if he's alive. It's her I'm worried about."

His voice was listless. He talked on simply because he could think of nothing else to do. "It's all my fault. I was insanely jealous of her and insulted her viciously. I wanted to get Courtney and I think I've succeeded. Then, of all guys, she gets tangled up with Courtney. I heard that his Chinese chauffeur drove her . . ."

He jumped to his feet. "Chinese chauffeur." He shrieked the words at the Chief.

Two detectives burst into the room revolvers drawn. They looked at Jimmy with apprehension.

"That's it, Chief," the reporter shouted, "they're headed for Chinatown! C'mon." He dashed from the room. Lawson nodded to the detectives to follow. They caught up with him as he dashed out of the side door.

The three piled into a waiting squad car and, siren screaming, headed toward Lagauchetiere Street.

Jimmy was out of the car before it came to a halt at the Clarke Street corner. He ran into one of the narrow doorways that line the street, up three flights of rickety stairs and burst into a fan tan game scattering cards and players alike.

He seized one of the men by the lapels of his coat. "Where is Kuo?" He shook the man violently.

The man didn't answer. Jimmy turned to the rest of the players only to be met by a sea of impassive Oriental faces. No one spoke.

He ran down the stairs leading from the rear of the room hopped a low fence and dashed into the kitchen of the Yan

Tung Cafe. Yan was stirring a huge cauldron of savoury soup when Jimmy came in. If he was surprised it did not show on his flat yellow face. "Have you seen Kuo, Yan?" Jimmy spoke softly to his friend.

"No Mister Holden."

"Are you sure, Yan?"

Yan reached back to the shelf and picked up a saucer. Jimmy stopped him. "You don't have to take an oath by breaking crockery, Yan, I believe you."

He left the restaurant and walked slowly east on Lagauchetiere. The night was unbearably warm and it seemed every resident of Montreal's Chinatown sat outside their dingy stores or on the balconies of their equally dismal homes.

The street was a myriad of signs. Chinese characters spelled out restaurant names. Papers were pasted on the brick walls and served as newspapers. Black clad figures shuffled in and out of the many cafes and gambling places.

Jimmy, his hands thrust deeply into his pockets, returned to the Clarke Street intersection and sat gloomily in the detectives' squad car. The two officers were absent but Jimmy thought he saw them posted at strategic positions along the short narrow strip of pavement which makes up the Chinese settlement.

He sat listening to the police calls for word of the chase. His hunch that Courtney would make for Chinatown was based solely on the fact that Kuo was with him. Once they managed to reach this section chances of catching them would be remote. There were passages between the houses plus underground exits in this area known only to a few Chinese and to practically no Occidental.

He first saw the car as it crossed St. Lawrence Main, a block away. It passed between the brilliant signs on either corner and picked up speed. Jimmy kicked the scout car to life and swung the wheel hard.

For a brief instant he saw Gisele before her hands raised to shield her face against the inevitable crash.

Time stood still, then the quiet air of Chinatown was shattered as the two cars collided with a sickening thud of twisting steel and splintered glass.

CHAPTER EIGHTEEN

Gisele's head was throbbing painfully as she awoke. She found herself in the front seat of the convertible which was travelling, she knew, north of St. Denis.

Courtney was driving, his handsome face set and hard. She turned slightly and felt a metal object jab at her right shoulder. Kuo was behind her. His gun blocked her chance of escape through the side door.

She tried to feign sleep but Kuo nudged her, with the gun.

"What did you do with them?" Courtney flung the words out.

"With what?" She found it difficult to speak. Her jaw ached and again she remembered Jimmy hitting her.

Kuo's gun poked her. "The jewelry I gave you. Where is it?" Courtney's patience was at a low ebb. He took one hand off the wheel and grabbed her wrist in a vise-like grip.

She winced in pain and tried to twist the door handle. Kuo rapped her sharply on the shoulder and she drew away.

The wail of a siren caused Courtney to release his hold. Kuo stared out of the rear window. "They are about two blocks away, Sir, just about crossing Jean Talon."

Courtney stepped hard on the gas and the car leaped forward. He pumped the brakes again and swerved east on Cremazie almost overturning the car. It righted itself after weaving crazily toward the opposite curb.

The siren grew louder when they reached St. Hubert Street. Gisele screamed as Courtney barely missed a north-bound truck which shot across the intersection.

Near Papineau, Courtney suddenly braked that car and turned into an alleyway opening off Cremazie. The car's headlight glared against a brick wall some 40 feet away. Courtney cursed and switched off the lights as the police car, siren blaring, sped by.

He turned in his seat and slapped Gisele across the face with back of his hand. "Where are they?"

She reeled under the blow and her head jerked back. Courtney struck her again and she felt a warm trickle of blood oozing down her chin.

Kuo reached from the rear seat and clutched her throat. She managed a high pitched scream before her breath was choked off. Her nails ripped into his hands and she fought to retain consciousness.

Her screams aroused the occupants of nearby flats. Lights flashed on and people began to pour on to rear balconies.

A man in shirt sleeves vaulted a fence and ran toward Gisele's side of the car. He reached for the handle just as Courtney started backing to the street. Gisele tried to catch the man's outstretched hand but Kuo leaned between them and brought his gun across the man's face. Blood ran between his fingers as the man crumpled to his knees holding a smashed nose.

Cries of "Police" went up from a dozen throats as Courtney, driving like a madman, scattered curious pedestrians and drove east again on Cremazie.

Gisele sobbed with terror. Courtney's face was a mask of hatred. Without warning he struck her again. "You bitch," he shouted.

The car reached Delorimier Avenue without mishap. Driving slower to prevent suspicion, he spoke softly to Kuo in a language Gisele did not understand. She heard the word "Lagauchetiere" and knew they were discussing Chinatown.

She looked frantically about for means to escape. Kuo twisted his fingers around the neck of her dress twisting it to form a garrotte around her throat. She found she could not move without cutting off her breath.

They turned west on Sherbrooke and had almost reached

Papineau, four blocks away, when Kuo spotted the police car. It was headed east and they could see a uniformed constable leaning out of the driver's window pointing at them.

Gisele heard the order to stop over the roar of the convertible's engine. Courtney heard it too. He kicked the car into a vicious leap forward just as a spider's web appeared on the windshield.

"They're shooting." He screamed and crouched over the wheel. The car turned south on Papineau, tires shrieking. He drove through a red light and Gisele heard a crash behind her as drivers sought desperately to get out of his path.

The wailing of the police siren brought all traffic to the curb clearing a way for Courtney as well as the police. He drove huddled over the wheel. His teeth were bared and a fleck of froth appeared at the corner of his mouth.

The speedometer clocked 72 as they passed Papineau Square and headed into the factory district. As the car screeched around corners and righted itself on Notre Dame Street, Gisele tried once more to free herself from Kuo's suffocating grip. He twisted her dress noose-like and she was forced to gasp for breath.

They roared over the bridge beside Place Viger Station and into the narrow streets of the old section. Courtney slowed the car only to turn corners. Beside the Old Court House the car swerved to the right, then to the left as they passed through Dead Man's Curve.

They were in the financial section. The streets were deserted except for a stray charwoman on her way to one of the office buildings.

The police car hove into view before they heard the siren. Gisele saw a puff of smoke as one of the policemen fired a warning shot. She saw Kuo's gun come up and explode close to her ear. Her head rang with the shot and acrid smoke stung her nostrils and eyes.

Courtney turned north, crossed Craig Street and drove into the heart of the former Red Light District. Here the narrow tortuous streets made driving even more hazardous. Realizing the police could easily throw a dragnet around this sector, Courtney looked for a road out.

He chose Charlotte Lane. Swinging the car he first hit Berger Street, then de Bullion and finally came out on Lagauchetiere Street, heading west.

He passed the hospital and looked at the single street separating them from Chinatown. The car zoomed across St. Lawrence Main. Kuo increased his grip on Gisele's dress and held the door handle. Courtney drew his gun and sat ready to make a run for it – shooting if necessary.

He turned to Gisele. "You will follow me – running. Kuo will be behind you in case you plan to escape. Don't stop when we are on the street or either one of us, probably both, will shoot you – immediately."

They had almost reached Clarke Street when they saw the car. It leaped at them at close range making a collision a certainty. Courtney made a futile attempt to avoid it by turning slightly to the right. He failed by a wide margin and the two cars came together with a sickening crash.

CHAPTER NINETEEN

Jimmy forced himself to relax as the cars crashed. He felt his body being thrown against the opposite door then out into the street.

He rolled over and over in the dust until the curbstone jammed against his body. He raised himself on one knee and shook his head savagely to clear away the dulling shock.

Courtney's figure ran past him as he drew himself to his feet. He started running in pursuit before he realized it, and was some ten feet from Courtney when the latter stopped and levelled his gun.

Jimmy threw himself through the air football fashion as a pistol barked. The two went down, Courtney's back hitting a fire hydrant as they did so. Jimmy felt a warm sticky mess spurting on his face. He wiped it from his eyes just in time to see Courtney's gun drop from lifeless fingers. He was shot squarely through the Adam's apple.

Jimmy reeled in a daze as a detective steadied him and began wiping the gore from his face. "That was pretty close, kid."

Jimmy gazed in fascination at the blood which covered his hands and suit. The detective spoke again. "We got the Chinaman too. He's winged badly but he'll live."

"Gisele!" Jimmy shouted and shaking himself free ran back to the smashed cars. He scrambled around the police cruiser to the convertible and looked in.

It was empty.

No one in the rapidly growing crowd had seen a girl. An intern from the nearby hospital tried to take him to a waiting ambulance. He brushed the white-clad figure aside and ran into the Yan Tung Cafe.

Yan welcomed him again without the slightest show of surprise. He beckoned him to the kitchen where he handed him a towel and some soap. Yan had not seen a girl leave the car in the excitement, nor had he heard any of his customers mention her, although the collision and gun fire was the sole topic of conversation in the cafe.

Jimmy called a cab and went back to *The Chronicle* office to write the story. His blood stained suit caused little comment except for a sarcastic observation from Beak Nose who wondered aloud if "Beau Brummel got into a brawl."

Jimmy didn't answer. He sat at his desk and pieced the story together. "An unidentified girl, believed to have been a passenger in the wrecked car, left the scene shortly after the crash. Police are seeking her for questioning." He read the words over as a lump formed in his throat.

For a moment he wanted to pencil the phrase out but thought better of it. He hastily drank a cup of coffee handed to him by a copy boy then brought the story over to Beak Nose.

The tall, lanky editor read it with no sign of emotion. He crossed out a word here, added another there, then sent it to the composing room. He poured Jimmy a tall drink from a bottle he kept in his drawer and leaned back in his chair.

Jimmy tasted the drink and pushed it away. "Why don't you keep beer in here? You know I can't drink that crap."

The editor ignored the question. "Any idea where to find the girl?"

Jimmy nodded sadly. "I think I know where she is."

The editor picked up the drink Jimmy refused, downed it in one gulp and turned to him. "Go home and get some sleep or go out and get drunk. I'll put Peterson on the story from here on."

Jimmy called a cab and leaned against *The Chronicle* Building while waiting for it to arrive.

Back in his apartment he stripped off his clothes, soaked in the bath for a good hour then donned a dressing gown and sat on the side of the bed drinking beer. He ached in every joint of his body and felt a stiffness working itself up from his knees.

He was a trifle sad about the Courtney case closing. It had been his story all the way. He was the first to dig it up, had followed it through seven months of hard work, then got in at the finish. And what a finish!

The main tip had come from Ray, the piano player. His addiction was a sore point with Jimmy who had continually suggested cures and treatments until Ray pleaded to be left alone.

The sudden wave of hatred for Courtney subsided as he realized there was nothing left to hate. He recalled the blood spurting from his throat and cursed vehemently as he realized it had stained his suit.

He wondered idly if bloodstains could be removed from the material. Making a mental note to call his tailor in the morning he poured himself another drink.

Sammy and Diane came in together. Jimmy looked closely at the girl. "Got a night off, Honey?"

Sammy answered for her. "The club is closed. There's a couple of cops stationed outside the door turning people away. I guess they are waiting for someone to show up."

Jimmy's voice almost broke as he said, "And I think I know who that someone is."

"Gisele?" Diane was obviously frightened.

Jimmy nodded.

Sammy rose, stretched and counted the bills in his pocket. "Writer's cramp is what you get trying to eat on a reporter's salary. And, Pretty Puss," he turned to Diane, "Today being novelty night – pay night – suppose we go to The Breakers and drink our fool heads off."

Diane turned to Jimmy. "C'mon James, you too."

He protested for a minute then dressed and joined the others in a booth. Sammy's conversation sound even more strained.

The Breakers was surprisingly empty of newspapermen. Big Jim explained that everybody from the publishers to the copy boys were working on the Courtney story.

Jimmy thumbed a nickel in the juke box before joining the others in a booth. He sat dejectedly sipping beer as the record played "Clair de Lune."

Big Jim motioned him to come into the bar. He rose wearily and accepted a drink before sitting on the small desk near the beer cooler.

"What's on your mind, Pig?"

Big Jim looked at him through narrowed eyes. "Eatin' yah heart out. Aintcha?"

"Shaddap."

"I know where the doll is at. Interested?"

Jimmy jumped from the cooler and grasped Schultz's arm. "Where?"

"At Lawson's office."

Without a word Jimmy ran from the cafe and jumped into Mike's cab which had just drawn up to the door. "Police headquarters!" Jimmy shouted.

Mike swung the cab in a U-turn startling everyone within two blocks then, leaning on the horn, cleared traffic from the street.

CHAPTER TWENTY

Gisele held her hands palms outward as the cars crashed. Kuo's hold on her dress served to lessen the force with which she was thrown forward. The dress ripped and she was free.

Neither Courtney nor Kuo seemed concerned about her as she slid from the car. The door on her side was smashed open offering her her first chance of escape. Quickly she rolled out of Courtney's line of vision to the rear of the car.

The men, she saw, were running leaving her on the crowded street. She picked herself up and walked slowly toward St. Lawrence Main.

Finding a drug store she explained to the clerk that she had fallen and wished some safety pins to make necessary repairs.

He smiled obligingly and led her to the rear of the store where she washed her face and removed her torn stockings. Five minutes later she emerged with her torn dress pinned back at the neck and the dust of the street brushed from it.

She walked north on St. Lawrence grateful that her appearance didn't attract attention. She hadn't the slightest idea of where she was going. She felt lost without her handbag which she dimly remembered having left at Jimmy's apartment.

She found some change under a ball of Kleenex in the pocket of the dress. Diane must have forgotten about it, she thought.

She was incapable of making any definite plans. Her jaw hurt and her head throbbed. Staying as long as she dared in the restaurant without raising suspicions, she left and walked north toward the Coq d'Or.

Turning the corner she stopped abruptly. Police were on guard at the entrance to the club and a curious crowd had gathered on the sidewalk.

She quickly retraced her steps back to St. Catherine and entered a small hamburger stand. She was beyond panic. The thought of going home filled her with remorse. Facing her parents would be a more difficult task then facing the police.

She threw the last of the change on the counter and set off for police headquarters.

The sergeant at the desk looked at her with open suspicion. Why did she want to see the chief of detectives personally? Did she think that anyone could walk in here and demand to see Mr. Lawson just like that? He snapped his fingers.

Wearily she explained that she wanted to talk about the Courtney case. The sergeant's face changed immediately and he ushered her into Lawson's office.

Lawson said nothing. He leaned his giant frame back in his swivel chair and waited for her to talk.

When at last she did he didn't interrupt. She told him of how she first met Courtney and the subsequent job at the club. Her relations with Jimmy and their disagreement over Courtney's attentions to her. She spoke rapidly about the events which led up to the collision in Chinatown.

A sergeant, she noticed, was taking down her statement. When she had finished she looked miserably at Lawson. "That's about all I know, Sir."

Lawson nodded and thanked her. "You can go now Miss Lepine."

Astonished she looked at him and wondered if she had heard right. "You mean you are not going to lock me up?"

The inspector grinned broadly. "We have no charge against you. I would suggest, however, that in the future you choose your playmates more carefully. And," he added, "don't leave town."

She nodded dumbly and left the office.

Walking once more on St. Catherine Street her spirits

sank as low as they possibly could. She felt very much alone and too miserable to care about the future. This, she thought, was the end of a dream.

Now that the danger of arrest was over she abandoned all thought of returning to the farm. She would get a waitress job and save enough money to go to some other city, Toronto, perhaps. Although she remembered Jimmy's expression that the city was "nowhere."

She walked as far as Diane's apartment feeling as if she were in a daze. Trixie's stout boy friend opened the door and Gisele saw most of the chorus with their boyfriends sprawled around the tiny apartment.

For lack of a better greeting she said, "Hello."

There was a heavy silence in the room and questioning stares seemed to bore through her. Trixie rose and walked over. "Kid, you look as if a drink wouldn't do you a bit of harm."

Gisele felt faint. She fingered the torn dress and just managed to say, "I'm sorry about the dress there was an accident and . . ." She fell into the arms of Trixie's boyfriend.

When she came to she found herself lying on the divan, a sea of faces looking down at her. Someone had placed a damp towel over her head and the coolness was soothing.

"I . . . I'm sorry," she mumbled.

Trixie handed her a drink and she immediately felt better. Sympathetic eyes grew wide with wonder as she described the wild ride through the city.

With a rare show of tact no one mentioned Jimmy. She had hoped someone would eventually volunteer some information about him. But no one mentioned him.

Excusing herself she went to the wardrobe and took her own dress from the floor and retired to the shower to change. She let the cold water spray over her body then rubbed herself briskly with a coarse towel until her skin tingled.

She then called Mike at The Breakers and asked him to pick her up. The conversation meanwhile had switched from the escapades of the evening to the possibility of getting paid by the club now that the bossman was no longer capable of making up the payroll.

"What do you think is going to happen, Gisele?" Trixie sounded worried.

"I do not know now," Gisele answered. "I will try and contact his lawyers and see what is to be done."

Mike entered the room quietly hand outstretched. Someone placed a drink in it and his smile stretched from ear to ear. "Never ask normal people." His accent was as thick as the soup of his native land.

Gisele waited until he finished his drink then followed him to his cab. "I do not have any money, Mike. Will you trust me for a short time?"

"Don't worry about it, Baby."

She gave him the address of Courtney's apartment. Mike made no comment until they were parked on the driveway. "Want I should wait?"

"No, thank you, Mike."

Therese opened the door for her and immediately fell on her neck crying bitterly.

Gisele pushed her away and walked into her bedroom. She took her luggage from the top shelf of the closet and began clearing out the drawers of her dresser.

CHAPTER TWENTY-ONE

She had almost finished packing when a police knock sounded on the door. Therese, her eyes still bloodshot and swollen, hurried to answer.

It was Gerard Daignault. Gisele recognized him as being one of the two men with whom Courtney had been sitting when she paid her last visit to the exclusive club.

She knew him to be one of Courtney's lawyers. He carried a briefcase and with sympathy showing in every line on his face, he extended his hand.

"I am most grieved, *Mam'selle*." His voice carried a tone of unmistakeable sincerity. "You have indeed had a most trying experience."

She motioned him to a chair and instructed Therese to bring drinks.

Daignault placed the briefcase on the coffee table, settled back in the chair. "Realizing how upset you must be I will be as brief as possible. In fact, I would not bother you at this moment were it not that various interests must necessarily be kept in operation. As it is at present, several decisions are to be made. You must make them."

Gisele stared with surprise. "I?"

Daignault shook his head solemnly. "It is against all professional ethics, Miss Lepine, but I must inform you, unofficially of course, that you are the sole benefactor of Monsieur Courtney's will. He had it drawn up the night we met at his club."

"But . . . but I want nothing. I will not accept anything." Gisele's head began to swim and her voice trailed off as she tried to explain the trouble and danger Courtney had brought her.

"Nevertheless," the lawyer continued, "you remain as sole benefactor for the moment. What you plan to do with the estate you can do when it is officially turned over to you. I, as executor, must work with you until such time as the will is declared legal and acceptable."

"Did . . . did he leave much?" She felt ashamed as soon as she asked the question.

"Considerable." He delved into the briefcase and handed her a long manila envelope. "This," he said, "was left with me with instructions to turn it over to you in case of a serious accident. I believe that today's happenings can be considered as such."

She ripped open the envelope and extracted a thick bundle of currency. She stared fascinated at the wealth. Daignault seemed unconcerned. "There should be some five thousand dollars. The sum is not included in his willed estate. He merely took precautions that you would be provided for in the event of a delay in executing his will."

Gisele placed the envelope on the arm of her chair. She looked in amazement as the lawyer listed Courtney's holdings and checked them off with a pencil. He figured busily for some time then said to her. "I would suggest you re-open the club tomorrow night."

"The girls are worried about the salaries and I guess that would be a wise move."

"As probably you know, Miss Lepine, the license of the club is not in Monsieur Courtney's name. It is in mine. I also have a small share."

"That I did not know – but it makes little difference."

"We will, therefore, give instructions to re-open bar at noon tomorrow and present the regular performance tomorrow night. You, of course, cannot appear with the show."

"But then we'll be short a girl." She protested.

"Not quite. The girls will work without a day off. Actually, the club being closed takes care of that one day off per week union regulation. Before the end of the week we shall bring in a girl from New York."

He reached for the phone and called the club. A worried janitor promised to relay instructions to the manager and everyone else concerned.

The lawyer grunted further instructions regarding the information to be given to the press then hung up.

Turning to Gisele he said. "There are other interests to be attended to. These I am afraid are not quite so pleasant as the operation of the cabaret."

Gisele only half heard his words. She was wondering what explaining to do to Jimmy – why, by this time, he probably didn't care anyway.

Wearily she asked, "What interests?"

The lawyer avoided her eyes for a second. "Perhaps it would be a wiser move on my part to bring you to them and let you see for yourself."

She nodded and followed him to the door.

They both sat in the front seat of Daignault's car and Gisele saw Mike leaning nonchalantly against the building. He waved casually to her as they drove away.

The lawyer headed the car east on Sherbrooke until crossing Park Avenue then turned north on one of the side streets. He stopped before a three-storey home set far back from the street. Getting out of the car he beckoned her to follow him.

Puzzled she mounted the stairs and waited as he rang the bell. His fingers beat out a rhythm on the on the button like a telegrapher fingering a telegraph key.

The curtains parted slightly and the face of a dark, elderly woman peered out for only an instant. The door fell back and closed rapidly after them. Gisele found herself in a large room which somehow resembled the lobby of a third-rate hotel.

Daignault and the woman were in deep conversation speaking in too low a tone for her to hear. She was wondering why the house needed so many chairs and divans when Daignault asked her to follow him.

He walked through the room into a narrow hallway and into a larger room. Gisele looked about with admiration. A thick rug covered the floor and silk drapes hung from the windows blotting out all but a small patch of subdued light. Here again there were many chairs and divans. The lamps, she noticed, were expensive and gave off a low blue light.

Daignault motioned her to a seat. The woman pulled a silken rope and she heard a faint gong being sounded somewhere in the upper part of the house.

A few moments passed in silence. Gisele folded her hands in her lap and waited expectantly. Soon the drapes closing off the door on the right parted and eight young girls entered single file.

Gisele gasped. Not one was over twenty years old. Each was clad in a chiffon negligee which barely concealed their youthful bodies. They paraded slowly before Gisele's horrified gaze.

She jumped to her feet, "*C'est un bordel!*"

Daignault rushed to calm her. The girls drew back in fright. Only the woman seemed composed. Hurriedly she shepherded the girls back upstairs then ran to a cabinet and brought brandy and glasses.

Gisele drank the fiery liquid thirstily. "This,' she stammered at the lawyer, "is a brothel. Why did you bring me here?"

Daignault drew his hands across his forehead in a helpless gesture. "They are . . . this is yours. It is part of the estate."

Gisele turned to the woman. "You will close this place now. It is no longer in operation."

The woman threw up her hands in horror. "*Mais Mam'selle . . .*"

Gisele's angry voice shouted at her. "You will close immediately or I will have the police close it."

She walked through the hallway to the front door. Daignault ran after her and joined her in the car.

CHAPTER TWENTY-TWO

They drove in silence to Sherbrooke Street. The thoughts of being proprietor of a house of ill-repute filled her with repulsion. She hardly noticed that Daignault had wheeled the car into the driveway of the club in which she had first met him.

Without comment the two walked into the tiny bar and sat at a corner table. The waiter bowed and Gisele ordered a beer. Daignault ordered a double scotch and swallowed half before speaking to her.

"*Mam'selle* Lepine." His voice sounded tired. "I hope you realize that I am only doing that which I was hired to do. I did not know that you were unaware of so many things. I suspected, yes, but did not know. It was easier to show you than to explain." He turned back to his drink.

Her voice was even. "How many such places do . . . are there?"

"Two others. That one is by far the most elaborate."

"I want the other two closed as well. Now!"

He looked at her as if to protest.

"Now!" she repeated hotly.

He nodded and walked to the telephone frantically thumbing a notebook. She watched him closely as he made two calls before returning to the table.

"They are closed," he said simply and resumed his seat.

"Are there other places of similar type, Mr. Daignault?"

He looked at her and smiled sadly. "No. Thank God."

They looked at each other and laughed aloud.

"Tell me Mr. Daignault. Have you ever been to The Breakers?"

He looked at her in surprise. "Me? Visit The Breakers?

Isn't that the place where prizefighters and other persons of that type congregate? No, I am sorry, I have not been to The Breakers."

"Well let us go there – I would appreciate a more cheerful place than this." She smiled at his injured dignity.

The lawyer looked ill at ease as Big Jim hugged Gisele when they entered the club. "Glad to see you Baby. Had yourself a time, huh?" He jerked his head in the direction of the uncomfortable Mr. Daignault. "Who's the schmoe?"

Gisele introduced them with some misgivings. She could see the pained expression on the lawyer's face as Schultz shook his hand.

The big man steered them to a booth and sat opposite them. He looked steadily at Daignault. "What's your racket, Bum?"

The lawyer made an attempt to protest but failed miserably. "I'm a lawyer," he answered as if ashamed of the fact.

"You her lawyer?" He clasped Gisele's hand.

"Yes."

"Ever go to the fights?"

"Never."

"Don't know what you're missing. Why I have a boy going to kill some jerk." Then he crushed two tickets into the lawyer's hand.

"You be there, see?"

Gisele sat quietly enjoying the conversation. She knew from Daignault's expression that he would move heaven and earth to be at the fights tomorrow. He was probably too frightened to do otherwise.

Daignault gave an audible sigh of relief as Big Jim returned to the bar. As he did so Gisele noticed Sammy coming through the door.

"This," she thought to herself, "is all Daignault needs."

Sammy spotted them and came over immediately. He

kissed Gisele French-fashion on both cheeks. "Baby, I've been looking all over town for you. Where've you been?"

She ignored his question and introduced Daignault.

Sammy looked him up and down. "A legal eagle, huh? Chased any interesting ambulances lately?"

Even Daignault smiled.

Gisele told Sammy to notify Diane that the club would re-open the next day if she had not already heard the news. She finished her drink and left with Daignault.

Sammy headed for the bar with an "I'm gonna borrow ten 'till payday" look in his eyes.

They were in the car before Daignault spoke. "A very, very peculiar place. Do you come here often Miss Lepine?"

"I met Courtney here," she replied in a flat voice.

"I understand," he said softly.

They drove back to her apartment and settled down once more with the coffee table between them. The lawyer spread numerous papers on it and drearily repeated the number of holdings, properties and enterprises which made up the estate of Gaston Courtney, deceased.

Gisele slumped back in her chair only half-listening. Her thoughts went racing back to less complicated days when she and Jimmy, along with Diane and Sammy had laughed their way through the pleasant nights.

She wondered if she would ever return to the chorus. Sadly she guessed she wouldn't. The few nights she danced with the line were the happiest in her life and she stowed them carefully in her chest of pleasant memories.

Remembering their episode with Sammy caused her to regret not having asked him for the loan of his key to the Shuter Street apartment. After all her request was legitimate, she reasoned. Her hand bag was still there to her knowledge.

The possibility of running into Jimmy prevented her from calling The Breakers and relaying her wish to Sammy.

The thought of Jimmy sent her into a melancholy mood. She wished Daignault would cease his lengthy report and go away.

If only she were free of all entanglements she would go home. She recalled bitterly that only a short time ago she intended returning to work as a waitress and had decided against admitting defeat and returning to the farm.

She let her mind review the pleasant aspects of the farm. No doubt she could return to the lodge. The owner had told her so when she left. Once there she could find peace. The family would be happy to see her. Perhaps even Pierre.

Seriously she tried to convince herself that, were it not for the present situation, she would return home. She felt elated with the prospect. The family . . . the friends she had made while at the lodge . . . everybody would be there. Everyone, she thought, sadly, but Jimmy.

She decided she was very tired.

CHAPTER TWENTY-THREE

Jimmy slowly walked down the stairs leading from Police Headquarters. He couldn't remember ever having felt so dejected. His only consolation was that Gisele wouldn't disobey Inspector Lawson's orders to remain in the city.

"So she's still in the city," he thought grimly, "and so are a million and a half other souls – plus a few heels." He walked slowly across Champs de Mars, deserted now except for the occasional panhandler from Craig Street or Skid Row as he had described it a score of times in his feature stories on the city.

Passers-by stared at him curiously as he thought aloud: "Well what did you expect Chump. First you insult her . . . then you accuse her . . . then you pop her on the kisser knocking her cold. Now suddenly you want to hold her in your arms. Brother, are you out of your stinkin' mind?"

He was still mumbling to himself when he reached Bleury Street. A taxi skidded to a stop inches from him. The driver pushed his head out of the cab. "Hey stupid, wanna get yahself kilt?"

Jimmy awoke from his daze with a start. He looked at the cab for an instant then calmly opened the rear door and climbed in. "Drive me to the Bohemian Club on Guy Street – and I agree with you. I am stupid." He slouched down in the seat.

The Bohemian Club is a walkup nitery just above St. Catherine Street. It boasts – but not too loudly – of having one of the best-known street numbers in the city. Citizens have long since given up counting the amount of times it has been re-decorated.

When Jimmy walked in it was sporting a super modern look. The owners had let a youthful genius run riot with his ideas plus a sizeable crew of workmen. The ultimate result being that the place closely resembled an expensive hat shop.

Jimmy climbed wearily onto a bar stool and slowly drank the cool beer that was almost immediately set before him. He emptied the bottle and held his head in his hand resting the elbow firmly on the bar.

The understanding bartender brought him another bottle. Jimmy drank this one faster than the last. The bartender looked at him curiously but said nothing. He brought another bottle.

Three hours later Jimmy was as drunk as he had been in some time. "I'm going to apply for a job as a copy boy on the East Labrador Weekly Blah – you see if I don't." The bartender suggested that it was a very noble newspaper famed for its active interest in civic affairs.

Jimmy thanked him, paid his bill and walked toward the door. He was surprisingly steady on his feet when turned to the bartender once more, "and if you're ever in East Labrador – look me up." Then he fell flat on his face.

Tiny devils were playing naughts and crosses on his brain with white-hot needles when he awoke. He groaned miserably and, after several efforts, managed to raise his head sufficiently to look around.

Through a haze he saw Sammy sitting in a chair opposite him then knew he was in the Shuter Street apartment. Sammy handed him a drink which he downed without tasting. It was tomato juice spiked heavily with Worcester sauce.

Sammy was talking in hushed, solemn tones ". . . and the wages of sin . . ."

"Shaddap. How did I get here?"

"Couple of cabbies cleaned you from the rug at the Bohemian Club. Boy, were you in fine shape. Whatever will the neighbors think?"

"To hell with the neighbors. You know what I think?"

"I can guess." Sammy went to the kitchen and brought out two bottles of beer.

Sammy uncorked the bottles and poured the drinks before clearing his throat and looking seriously at Jimmy. "Kid, I don't know how to say this but our term of sharing light housekeeping is just about kaput."

Jimmy gave him a crooked look. "What are you driving at?"

"You see, Diane and I were talking things over and we decided . . ."

"My God, no!"

"That's the way it is, Jimmy. We have an apartment and everything is set. The big day is set for about two weeks from now."

"Well, nothing lasts forever, does it Sammy?"

"No, I guess not."

"It's been fun. Let's not get sentimental and sticky-like."

"Let's go out and get stiff instead, huh?"

"How about Diane?"

"I explained that you and I would no doubt go out and get plastered so she stayed home to do her hair, write letters and stuff like that there."

"So what are we waiting for?"

A week later Sammy moved his belongings amid much celebration. Two taxi drivers pressed into service as movers spent their time transporting luggage, books, suits, and tipsy guests between two widely-separated apartments.

To facilitate the procedure Sammy had thoughtfully set up a bar in each apartment. As a result willing, although unsteady, hands carried his worldly goods from bar to taxi to bar to taxi to bar. It was all very pleasant.

Within a short time the shuttle service lacked drivers and frantic phone calls were made to replace hackies no longer able to see clearly.

The move made history of sorts and was thereafter referred to as "The Retreat From Shuter Street."

As Sammy made the final trip Jimmy handed him Gisele's handbag with instructions to forward it to her through Diane.

The apartment seemed strangely empty with Sammy gone. As the days passed Jimmy found himself spending less and less time in the place and more and more time in the countless bars with which he was so familiar.

He found himself losing interest in the newspaper business and often considered joining Tyler in Miami. One night he went as far as to wire his friend asking the possibilities of tying on with a paper there. Next day Tyler wired back. "Sober up. It is bad enough with hurricanes without you arriving on the scene."

CHAPTER TWENTY-FOUR

The days seemed endless to Gisele. Although Inspector Lawson had told her she could leave town if she wished, that the police no longer needed her for questioning, she felt loathe to leave until Courtney's will had been officially read.

She tried to keep herself from thinking of the estate. The amount of money involved and the countless interests which would take up so much of her waking hours frightened her.

Suddenly wealth meant little. She would gladly have given everything to be back in her room on Dorchester Street looking forward to doing shows and meeting Jimmy. She hadn't seen nor heard from him since he struck her at the apartment.

Walking to the window she looked over the city not knowing whether she loved it dearly or hated it passionately. It had brought her everything she wanted and had taken away the one thing she loved but hadn't expected. How many others had looked at it with similar thoughts; how many others both hated and loved it. She couldn't even guess.

A knock on the door interrupted her thoughts. She opened it to admit Daignault and a rather shabbily dressed woman of uncertain age. Daignault was visibly agitated.

The woman looked ill at ease and stared first at Gisele then at Daignault as if uncertain of the reception she would receive.

Gisele stood aside as they entered. Daignault went immediately to the coffee table and spread out a sheaf of legal papers. The woman stood awkwardly near the door until he told her, rather sharply, to sit down.

"Perhaps an introduction is in order, Monsieur Daignault." Her voice carried a heavy tone of sarcasm.

Daignault looked nervously at Gisele. He coughed. "This is Mrs. Courtney." He jerked his head in the direction of the frightened woman.

"Mrs. Courtney?" Gisele almost collapsed with shock. She stared at the woman who cowered under her gaze.

The lawyer rustled the papers with trembling fingers. "She is willing to accept a small settlement and return home. She lives in the country . . . has a small chicken farm. Someone gave her a newspaper and she recognized Mr. Courtney's picture . . . he left her many years ago and threatened her if she followed him . . . she came searching for his grave . . . finally went to the police who sent her to me . . . she didn't identify herself at the station . . . no one knows who she is . . . that is, with the exception of ourselves."

"What settlement is she asking for?" Gisele could not take her eyes from the woman.

Daignault laughed ironically. "Bus fare home. Exactly $6.70."

"What are those papers for?" She pointed to the documents on the coffee table.

Daignault was unscrewing the top of his fountain pen. "She can sign these. They're not legal of course and wouldn't stand up in court – but I doubt if she understands that. We had better speak in English. She speaks only French."

Gisele walked quickly to the coffee table and scooped up the papers. Eyes blazing she tore up them to shreds as Daignault jumped to stop her.

She threw the fragments on the floor and ran to the woman. She threw her arms around her and hugged her affectionately. Speaking in French, she said, "Everything is yours. Everything. I want nothing."

Gisele sat beside the woman on the divan. Her attempts to comfort her were of no avail. The woman was sobbing violently and Gisele was at a loss as to which course to take. He offer of what was left of the five thousand Courtney had given her was tearfully refused.

Finally she stood staring at the woman defiantly. "What then," she asked coldly, "do you want of me?"

The woman stopped sniffling long enough to look beseechingly at her. Speaking in clipped French she said morosely. "I wish that you would stay here with me. I have no children of my own and I have been so lonesome . . ." He voice reached the whining stage before it broke.

Sympathy shone in Gisele's eyes as she looked at the sobbing creature. . . . She made a pitiful picture sitting there dejected although wealthy enough to enjoy the things of which she, too, had probably dreamed, just as Gisele had dreamed only a short time ago.

The woman's tears and supplications embarrassed her to such an extent that she excused herself and called Mike at The Breakers. Giving him her location she borrowed a line from Sammy's vocabulary. "For Christ's sake get me out of here."

She walked rapidly through the living room into her bedroom and quickly packed her things. Having done that she poured a glass of rye in anticipation of Mike's arrival.

The woman was still sobbing quietly. Gisele tried again to silence her. She felt thankful to the huddled form who arrived at the precise moment she, herself, had felt overwhelmed – and not a little unhappy at being the one, who, unwillingly, was chosen to carry on Courtney's affairs.

When Mike arrived she handed him the glass of rye without comment. His narrowed eyes took in the situation immediately and, having dashed off the whiskey in one gulp, set about moving her bags.

Without being told he drove her to a Peel Street hotel. She paid him in silence despite his protests and quickly followed the bellhop to her room.

Once inside she wandered about the spacious room wondering what to do next. Her window faced the mountain and the cross atop it was already alight. She gazed at it in admiration for some time before unpacking her bags and hanging her new gowns neatly in the closet.

On an impulse she called Diane. The chorine was making the best of her day off by trying to return to some semblance of order the apartment she was to occupy as Mrs. Sammy Hoffman.

"I am leaving for home tomorrow, Diane." Gisele made her decision as she talked to her friend. "I have had enough of the city. It wasn't made for me. Back home I will have a chance to forget . . . everything."

Diane's protestations were many. "But you have to stay for the wedding. You are to be a bridesmaid. Naturally, the best man will be . . ." She broke off hastily.

Gisele's heart felt heavy. "Nevertheless I am leaving on the morning bus, Diane. I am anxious to get home." She hung up shortly after Diane had uttered finally, though feebly, "Oh."

CHAPTER TWENTY-FIVE

It had been a big day for Jimmy. In an effort to forget the events of the past few days he had thrown himself at his typewriter and had written all the features he had intended writing for the past two months.

As his fingers steadily pounded the keys and the hands of the city room clock bore down on two a.m., Beak Nose walked over to him with a suspicious gleam in his eye.

"Look, Brisbane," the city editor's voice was sarcastic – but those who knew him well could have detected a minute note of kindness in it, "if you think you're going to be paid for the overtime you've put in – forget it. I don't know what cooks with you but I don't want you to get into the habit of this sort of thing. I'm off, so let's go out and have a fast one and you can tell me all your troubles and I promise not to listen."

He walked over to the closet and jammed a battered felt on his head and stood waiting while Jimmy slipped into his jacket.

They sat beside the juke box in The Breakers for some time before Beak Nose decided they should telephone Sammy. The call created considerable discussion at Sammy's end of the line but, after many promises – none of which he intended keeping – Sammy broke away from his soon-to-be bride. His arrival at The Breakers reminded old time newsmen of a long term convict finally getting his parole and seeking the outside for the first time in years.

He had barely ordered a drink when Diane's trim figure entered the club. She sat beside him and smiled sweetly. "Just in case, Darling."

An uneasy silence settled over the table. Each knew that the absent Gisele was the uppermost thought in each of their minds. Jimmy studied the label of a beer bottle as if waiting for someone to say something.

Beak Nose eventually broke the silence. His absurd face, creased with wrinkles left by 32 years in the newspaper business, looked desperately serious. His thinning hair was bordered by grey, giving the impression that someone had placed a bowl on his head then tinted grey the hair that was still exposed.

He coughed politely. "Years ago," his voice was strangely gentle, "I was a cub on a sheet out in the 'Peg. Was making a fast $12 per week – every week that is – and figured I was doing pretty well."

"Actually met a girl who could stomach my homely pan and all was simply ducky. She loved me – I loved her, and we swore eternal love come hell or missed deadlines."

Diane leaned forward in interest. "Then?"

Beak Nose took a healthy swig of his drink, leaned back in the chair and continued. "Then just as I had saved enough for the first instalment on the ring, she said I should go East. I was strictly a prairie boy at the time and couldn't see the wicked cities of Toronto or Montreal. Toronto I still can't see – but Montreal brother-r-r."

"Anyway she pleaded with me to better myself and I grew rather weary of her sermons. We had a battle – not a serious one, you understand, just a minor league spat."

"However she refused to speak to me after that. I used to hang around her house waiting for a chance to make like an unexpected meetin' – but no dice. She avoided me and I felt pretty miserable about the whole situation."

"One day I received an offer from *The Chronicle* and told all our mutual friends that I was leaving for Montreal. I figured that at least one of them would tell her and she'd come running back to me. It didn't work out that way, though."

"Came time for me to leave and I stood at Portage and Main hoping for at least a sight of her. She didn't show. I almost missed the train too."

"That was many years ago. Since then I heard the she married a clerk in a drug store and is now busily engaged in raising a family."

Diane's eyes were soft and sympathetic. "Do you miss her?"

"Not quite," Beak Nose answered gloomily. "But I haven't married for one reason, her. I keep telling myself that I am better off. No, I don't miss her. But when Fall goes in to bat for Summer and the leaves turn color – I wonder what she is doing. When the first snow flurries swirl along St. Catherine I think of Portage Avenue and how she used to huddle into her Hudson's Bay coat."

"No, I don't miss her. The only reason I have a subscription to the *Winnipeg Free Press* is because I like to look at the grain market reports. In fact, I get along without her very well – except sometimes."

No one spoke as the first rays of the morning sun came through the front windows of The Breakers painting a weird pattern of light on the floor. They were the last party in the club and Big Jim sat half asleep, cigar unlit and drooping, in a corner chair.

Diane looked wearily at Jimmy. "The bus for St. Christophe leaves in precisely seven minutes."

Jimmy looked at her. He was uncertain as to what she meant. Then, suddenly, he was on his feet and running from the club.

He was still running when he pushed his way through the revolving doors of the bus terminal. Desperately he looked around the nearly deserted waiting room. The soda fountain clerk looked at him through weary eyes. A few odd passengers relaxed sleepily on the long, wooden benches.

Jimmy's heart sank. Then, as if through a fog, the bus announcer's voice cut through the silence: "Leaving from

Bay Number Eight. Bus for Ste. Rose, Rosemere, Ste. Therese, St. Jerome. . . ."

Jimmy paused only momentarily. He dashed out onto the starting platform looking frantically for the bus. Finally he saw it at the extreme end of the platform.

He darted through the wearily waiting crowd, mumbling pardons as he ran. He cut rapidly down Bay Eight and savagely pulled at the now-closing door.

A startled bus driver half rose in his seat to protest but Jimmy had already entered the bus. He barged his way down the narrow aisle and pulled Gisele from her seat.

Her screams brought the driver at a run.

Jimmy felt himself grasped firmly from behind, but nevertheless, clung to her desperately. The driver, a husky, broad-shouldered knight of the road, pulled him easily to the front of the bus. Jimmy still clung to Gisele and the three-some reached the exit in that fashion.

Jimmy was trying to embrace her as the driver's frantic shouts for help were answered.

Finally she threw her arms around his neck and kissed him soundly. A group of drivers, dispatchers and porters looked on in amazement.

"I love you, Sugar Puss." Jimmy's voice broke like a twelve-year-old's.

She hugged him to herself hungrily. "Jimmy, Jimmy."

The bus driver pushed his cap to the back of his head. He leaned wearily against the side of his vehicle and watched them disappear into the brilliant sunshine of Dorchester Street.

SUGAR PUSS

ON DORCHESTER STREET

AL PALMER

WHEN THE SUN goes down and the neons go up Montreal becomes one of the world's most colorful cities. Through its countless night clubs, cocktail bars, lavish hotels and colorful streets pass a host of fabulous characters whose presence gives the city the atmosphere for which it is famous.

Into this pseudo-paradise came Gisele Lepine—fresh as the cool clean air of her Laurentian village and eager with the realization of a five-year dream—Montreal.

Gisele met the characters, basked in the synthetic glamor of the cabarets and reached the goal she had set as a climax to her personal five-year plan.

Few authors could capture the life and atmosphere of Montreal as does Al Palmer in SUGAR PUSS. He was born in the east end of the city and in fact celebrates his birthday (May 18th) on the same day as does his native city.

A former columnist on the Montreal *Herald*, he is considered an authority on the city. In this novel he takes his readers behind the scene of a metropolitan newspaper. He takes them backstage of the city's leading night clubs and introduces them to the fabulous characters he knows so well. This is the heart beat of a great city . . . this is a town caught with its inhibitions down . . . this is Montreal.

A News Stand Library Pocket Edition